Passionate Brew

An Enemies-to-Lovers Beach Town Brewery Romance

Sadira Stone

Sadira Stone

Contents

Chapter One

♥

"You can't be serious." Her dad's bad news bomb turned Lilo Eisinger's knees to jelly. She sank into a chair at her parents' kitchen table and brushed aside the road maps and KOA camping brochures. "I don't mind helping you at the brewery, but taking over?"

Her father enveloped her clenched fist in his broad, callused hand. "Lorelei, it's time. Doc says these long hours on my feet are destroying my back. Besides, I've been promising your mom a cross-country road trip for years. And after your Aunt Petra's passing, well—who knows how long we've got to enjoy each other's company?"

Guilt nibbled Lilo with needle-sharp teeth. Dad had earned his retirement after two decades as Salty Dog's head brewer. But the thought of facing Ryan Lee's smug face every day curdled her stomach. Though easy on the eyes, Dad's partner rubbed her every kind of wrong way possible. Always had.

She threw up her hands. "Talk about short notice, Dad. I just got home." For the past two months, she'd visited microbreweries up and down the West Coast, sampled products, interviewed brewers, and judged craft brew competitions. "Next week, I'm checking three potential brewery sites. I'm courting investors, finalizing my business plan..."

Dad patted her hand. "Punkin, Salty Dog is ripe for a new direction. Why not save yourself all the start-up costs and hassle? Put your training and experience to use right here."

She crossed her arms and scowled. "You just want to keep me in Trappers Cove."

"Of course we do." Mom set down three steaming mugs of tea, then sat beside her.

"But you're leaving," Lilo wailed, embarrassed by the childish whine in her voice.

Mom patted her hand. "We'll be back. TC will always be our home. And yours, we hope."

"But Salty Dog is too small for what I have in mind."

Dad raised a wiry eyebrow. "So build up the business until you have enough capital to expand."

Lilo glowered into her tea.

Her parents exchanged a knowing look. Mom squeezed her shoulder. "What's really bothering you?"

For their sake, she kept her language mild. "You know Ryan and I don't get along."

What a massive understatement. Like so many men in the brewing trade, Ryan Lee was a sexist swine, always monitoring her whenever she came in to help Dad—which happened more and more frequently since his back started acting up. She'd cut her European brewery tour short when muscle spasms landed Dad in the hospital, and how had Ryan thanked her? Constantly peering over her shoulder and questioning her decisions. Who needed that kind of macho bullshit? Especially from someone she'd known since middle school. So what if he grew up to be a handsome, well-dressed smooth talker?

Mom pushed back from the table with a sigh. "It's okay, Robert. We can delay our trip until you find another master brewer. Maybe that nice Marco kid? Or Mia?"

Dad shook his head. "They're not ready for the responsibility. Only Lilo has the expertise and experience we need." He scooted his chair closer and clasped her hand in both of his. "Darling girl, I've spent the past twenty years building that brewery. I can't just turn it over to someone I don't trust."

She squirmed as Dad's guilt knife slid between her ribs, aiming right for her heart.

"These days, the brewery can't keep up with demand," he continued. "This is the perfect opportunity for you." He leaned his elbows on his knees and fixed her with his pale gray gaze, so earnest and trusting. "Ryan's a good man, but he doesn't know half of what you do about brewing."

She glowered at her clenched fists and tried her damnedest to wrestle her resentment under control.

Dad squeezed her hand. "Tell you what, Punkin, I'll make a deal with you. Give Salty Dog a year. That'll give Ryan enough time to find another head brewer, if that's what you both want. In exchange, I'll invest in your own brewery."

She yanked her hand from his grip. "Dad, you can't." No way would she take start-up money from her blue-collar dad and retired schoolteacher mom. They'd worked too hard for their little nest egg, and at thirty-eight, she was too damn old to be mooching from her parents.

He waved away her protest. "I've got some money set aside. I hope I'll end up investing it in Salty Dog, but if you choose otherwise, I'll respect your choice."

Lilo pushed back from the table. "I need time to think."

"Fair enough." Dad slapped his thighs, then rose with a muffled groan. "Ryan's a schmoozer, but he's got a good heart. You two would make an excellent team."

Ouch. Clearly, her father viewed Ryan as the son he never had—impossible to miss the affection shining in Dad's eyes whenever he mentioned that pretty-faced prick.

Biting back her grumbles, she hugged her parents, then drove home. She craved a long walk on the beach to clear her head. Hopefully, the brisk March wind would blow away all the bullshit, leaving just the truth—a strategy that usually worked, though this knotty dilemma might require more than a little sea air to unclench its hold on her gut.

But when she returned to her front porch an hour later, hair windblown, cheeks salt-stung, bare feet coated with sand, the only clarity she'd found was how much she loved this place. Where else could an itinerant brewer afford a seaside cottage? Where else could she wake to the cry of seagulls and fall asleep to the surf's soft breath? And though she enjoyed travel, no hotel or short-term rental would ever match the comfort of her own home and the quirky little beach town where everyone had known her since childhood.

After rinsing her feet, she cracked a refreshing Belgian-style pale ale and sat on her deck, feet propped on her glass-topped fire table. While the flames warmed her toes, she gazed out at the swaying dune grass.

"Okay," she told the curious seagull perched on the deck railing. "Points in favor of Salty Dog." First, she wouldn't have to prove her craft brewer cred. The Salty Dog crew already knew her, and she enjoyed working with them—except Ryan, of course. Second, it would be great to spend more time with her hometown friends. Third, she loved a challenge, and if she could handle the know-it-all brewer bros she'd apprenticed under, she could damn well handle Ryan Lee. All she needed was firm boundaries. The brewery would be her domain, and the saloon would be his. Easy peasy.

One burning question remained—would Salty Dog's customers would go for the creative beers she wanted to brew? While bigger towns offered a ready consumer base for sophisticated craft beer, Trappers Cove was more traditional, less adventurous—especially now, during the off season.

But if she chafed at being underestimated, she shouldn't underestimate others, right? And Dad was correct about one point—a brewery that couldn't keep up with demand offered an excellent opportunity for growth. Why not add her own beers to the mix?

"Even smug-ass Ryan Lee would have to see the sense in that proposition. Right, bird?"

The gull squawked and flapped away.

"Yeah, well, what does a flying trash panda know about business?" She dug her phone from her pocket and addressed the flaming orange horizon. "Last chance, Universe. If this is a stupid idea, tell me now."

No reply came—just the soft sigh of surf and the seagulls' evening song.

She sucked in a deep breath of twilight calm before punching in Dad's number. "Okay. I'll do it. One year."

Relief lightened his gravelly voice. "I'm so glad, Punkin. I'll tell Ryan in the morning."

Her gut tightened. "You haven't told him yet?"

"I wanted to check with you first. Talk to you tomorrow." He ended the call with an ear-piercing smooch.

Lilo clutched her phone to her chest. Holy shit balls. She'd assumed Ryan had already agreed to Dad's scheme. What if he hated the idea? What if he capitulated out of guilt, and they had to endure an entire year shackled together?

This was going to be a nightmare.

Chapter Two

♥

Ryan Lee set his coffee mug on the balcony railing, laced his hands behind his head, and heaved a contented sigh. He cherished this moment of morning calm before his busy workday—and work night, usually. Though he had a great crew, he preferred to keep a sharp eye on all aspects of Salty Dog's daily operations, from bar to kitchen to brewery. A smart business owner should know his domain from top to bottom, and Ryan damn sure did.

The constant demands downstairs made this morning breather all the more precious. He'd considered buying one of those new condos facing the beach, but living above his workplace was too convenient to give up, even if the faint beer smell never really aired out. So what? Beer was his livelihood, his passion, his key to success. And thanks to Robert Eisinger, his trusty head brewer, he didn't have to make the stuff himself. Good thing, too, since his own brewer training was nearly two decades old.

After a good stretch, Ryan rose to face his workday, an easy smile on his face as he trotted down the staircase and through Salty Dog's back door.

Passing the glass wall that separated the brewery from the saloon, he raised a hand in greeting. Robert looked up from his clipboard and waved, a wide grin across his weathered face. Customers loved watching the handsome, silver-haired brewer supervise his young brewing minions.

Ryan was damn lucky that, when he purchased Salty Dog, Robert agreed to stick around. The previous owners were nice folks who loved beer but had zero business sense. Over the past ten years, Ryan built this place from a dumpy dive bar to the most popular nightspot in Trappers Cove, beloved by locals and tourists alike. Holding onto that top spot took constant vigilance.

Mia, one of the assistant brewers, perched on a ladder and cleaned the brewery window, her long braids swinging with each swipe of her Squeegee. "Mornin', boss," she chirped.

"Morning, sunshine. Did you guys figure out that problem with the pump?"

"Robert and Lilo are working on it."

"Cool. Thanks." *And thanks for the warning.*

Robert's stunning daughter Lilo hated Ryan's guts. Ever since seventh grade, when Dad died and Mom moved their fractured family to Trappers Cove, he'd crushed hard on the dramatic, dark-haired beauty with piercing gray eyes. Of course, she'd wanted nothing to do with the skinny, swim team nerd he was back then, and her feelings for him hadn't warmed one degree in the intervening twenty-six years. He'd learned to live with her hostility, though it still needled his ego. Besides, Lilo's visits were good for business. Guys flocked to Salty Dog to watch her graceful movements as she climbed ladders and peered into brewing kettles.

"Yo, Ry," Quinn called from behind the bar. "Package for you." Elbows-deep in suds, she tilted her chin toward a huge carton by the front door.

A wide grin stretched his lips. The octopus! He'd paid far too much for this fiberglass sculpture with light-up eyes, but from the moment he laid eyes on the kitschy sea beast, it was love at first sight, the perfect addition to the bar's collection of nautical knickknacks. Whipping out his pocket knife, he slit the packing tape, extracted the tentacled monster, and hoisted it overhead with a hoot. "Isn't she gorgeous?"

"Almost as pretty as you, kiddo." Wendy, Salty Dog's head cook, set a tray on the bar. "Where you gonna put it?"

"Over there, I think, to keep the mermaid company. We can hang daily special signs from its tentacles." He set the octopus down and followed his nose to Wendy's tray. "What have you got for us today?"

"Mack and I can't agree, so you decide. Which sauce you want for the halibut sandwich?"

He and Quinn dipped fries into each sauce while Wendy maintained a stony stare. His chef had strong opinions about flavors, and the Great Chowder Debacle had proved it was best not to cross her.

He shot Quinn a questioning glance, but she just shrugged.

"Okay, I like—" His finger hovered over one dish, then the other until he spotted the faint flicker that betrayed Wendy's preference. "This one."

The cook grinned and hollered, "Suck it, Mack. Cajun remoulade for the win." Waving like a beauty queen, she strutted back to her kitchen, her wide butt bouncing.

Quinn chuckled and hooked a thumb toward the entrance. "Propane hasn't arrived yet. Ernie was supposed to deliver at nine."

"Gah." Ryan stuffed a handful of fries into his mouth, then strode to his office. March nights were still cold enough to require heaters on the deck, and seats at the large fire table always filled up first.

After an hour of shuffling papers, making calls, and answering emails, he returned to the bar for a coffee and found his best friend

Jesse del Toro chatting with Quinn over a flat of fresh herbs from his farm east of town.

Jesse nodded toward the brewery in the back. "Look at the old dude polishing his beer tanks like they were classic cars."

Ryan tsked. "Kettles, not tanks. They're Robert's babies, all right."

"Speaking of babes, I see Lilo's back in town." Jesse gave a low whistle. "Don't know how you work with her without making a play."

"Watch out, now, or someone's gonna tell Gemma." Ryan liked Jesse's new girlfriend—great smile, bawdy sense of humor, and she got Jesse's fuddy duddy ass into party mode more often.

Quinn cocked her hip. "Lilo's too cute for Ryan."

"You just want her for yourself," Jesse parried.

"Maybe." Rocking from heel to toe in her shiny oxfords, Quinn snapped her paisley suspenders.

Jesse elbowed Ryan. "Better move fast, man. Quinn's way better looking than you."

Ryan's phone alarm pinged, saving him from further ribbing. "Excuse me. Got a meeting with my brewer."

Inside the brewery, Robert stood beside his coffee-break table. He gave Ryan a one-armed hug and a warm smile. "Have a seat, son."

Ryan nodded toward a third, empty chair. "Are we expecting someone?"

A flash of movement jolted him as Lilo stepped around one of the tall brew kettles. He'd forgotten to brace himself for impact.

They were both pushing forty now, so you'd think he'd be over this startle reflex, but those spooky eyes always got to him—pale gray irises ringed with slate, and a laser-sharp gaze that looked right through him.

Her long ponytail hung over her shoulder, its color dark and rich as porter. With a bold, unwavering stare, she grabbed a hank of hair in each hand, and yanked to tighten it. Might as well pound her chest. This beauty was prepared for battle.

Ryan arranged his face in a mask of nonchalance and rose to greet her. "Good to see you, Lilo."

She gave him a tight nod. "I'll get the samples." She stalked away, her spine as straight as his inconvenient erection. Good thing she only helped Robert periodically. Lusting after the daughter of his surrogate dad felt like a perverse betrayal.

He leaned onto his elbows and clasped his hands. "So, why the meeting?"

Lilo returned with three tall IPA glasses, each half full. She set them on the table, sat, and adopted a similar posture, her knuckles white as she regarded him through narrowed eyes.

What the hell did I ever do to you? And why do you even come here if you hate me so much?

Robert cleared his throat. "Just a little tweak to the hops mixture on the Salty Siren IPA. Makes the citrus flavor more pronounced. Tell me what you think."

Ryan sniffed, then sipped. "Nice. Refreshing." Honestly, he wasn't a hundred percent sure he tasted any difference. That's why he relied on Robert's sharp palate. The old man had never steered him wrong.

Robert grinned. "The change was Lilo's suggestion."

Heat flushed Ryan's face. Since when was Lilo interfering in her dad's recipes? Still, he'd better play nice in front of Robert, so he tipped his glass and gave her a lukewarm smile.

She folded her arms over her too-damn-interesting chest. "I judged a craft beer competition in Mendocino last month. The winning IPA used this mixture, as near as I can figure."

"Beer plagiarism?"

Her lip curled. "Don't be stupid. All brewers borrow ideas and inspiration. I've never laid eyes on their recipe."

Robert raised his hands, palms out. "Now, now. We're all just trying to make the best beer possible, right?" He gave each of them a pointed look.

Ryan forced a smile. "Of course we are." He touched Lilo's arm. "Sorry. I didn't mean to give offense."

Her gaze rose heavenward as if praying for help—or his demise.

Robert continued in a jovial tone. "You know, I've been working these kettles for over twenty years now. The past ten have been the best with you at the helm. You've done the brewery proud."

Genuinely touched but still suspicious, Ryan reached across the table and squeezed his mentor's arm. "Thank you. We make a good team."

Robert continued, "Did I tell you the Mrs. lost her sister last month?"

"No. I'm so sorry. Please give Olga my deepest sympathies."

"Thank you, son. I will." The older man leaned onto his elbows. "It got us to thinking. Life's too short. It's time we take that cross-country trip I've been promising her for years."

A strange tingling gripped the base of Ryan's skull. "You're taking some time off?"

"No, son. I'm retiring."

That tingle bloomed into goosebumps. Struggling to expand his vise-tight ribs, Ryan waited for the sweet old guy to grin and declare it all a colossal joke. How was he going to keep the brewery running without Robert? The rest of the crew were too green. None of them had Robert's finesse and deep well of brewing knowledge. Unless...

Oh no.

Robert beamed at his daughter. "Don't worry. Lilo has agreed to take the wheel."

As he and Lilo locked gazes, he had the strangest sensation, a full-body shiver—of warning?

Lilo's chest rose and fell. Her lips twitched.

She doesn't want this any more than I do.

Oblivious, Robert continued. "Lilo's the best craft brewer I know. There's no one I trust more to keep Salty Dog on course."

She closed her eyes and pinched the bridge of her nose.

Oh, this was bad. Very, very bad. But what choice did he have? Without Robert's help, Salty Dog would've flopped long ago. He had to honor the old guy's wishes. And Robert would never put Lilo in this position if she couldn't handle the job.

Not that he had anything against female brewers, but they were few and far between. Would the change in leadership affect his bottom line? Robert handled the brewery, but the responsibility for the whole business, from bar to kitchen to beer sales through-out the area, not to mention all the employees' livelihoods—that all fell squarely on Ryan's shoulders as owner and CEO of Salty Dog.

His old friend smacked the tabletop. "Well then, it's all settled. I'll leave on Friday."

So soon? Ryan fought a wave of nausea. Time to bottle up his personal feelings and focus on business. Besides, if Lilo ran into trouble, she could always call her dad. He rose from his seat and gave her the best smile he could manage. "Welcome aboard, Lilo. I'm glad to have your help."

They'd have a private word later to make sure she wasn't being railroaded into a job she didn't want. God knows what he'd do if she backed out.

For the next six hours, he snuck glances through the glass wall. Lilo must have ESP, because each time she'd spin around to stare back at him. So he resorted to hiding behind a potted palm like a kid playing detective. He spotted her chatting amiably with Marco and Mia, the young assistant brewers, and Madison, one of the local kids who helped with cleaning and hauling. No sign of snark or sniping, just relaxed interaction. Perhaps, given enough time and careful handling, he and Lilo could get to that place.

She whirled and glared in his direction.

"Shit," he hissed and ducked below the bar, bonking into Quinn's leg.

Startled, she sloshed beer on his head. "What the hell are you doing down there?"

He snatched a towel and blotted his dripping hair. "Checking the baseboards. You let your baseboards go, and before you know it, the whole place is falling down."

Quinn gave a snort. "You ever consider therapy?"

Later, around six, when he spotted Lilo pulling on her jacket, he trotted to intercept her. "Lilo, hang on."

She stiffened, jaw tight, gray eyes narrowed.

He sidled closer and lowered his voice. "Listen, is this job what you really want?"

She dropped her gaze with a sigh. "It's what my dad wants, and I want him to relax and enjoy his road trip with Mom. They've earned it, don't you think?"

"It's a very generous thing you're doing."

Her lips twisted in a humorless grin. "Yah. It is. But I don't mind doing this for them."

Her grim expression belied her words, but he had no doubt she loved her dad, and so did he. Having lost his own father at a young age, he'd latched onto the kindly brewer as a surrogate paternal figure. Losing him was going to hurt.

He cupped Lilo's elbow. "You know, once they leave, I could look for someone else."

"You don't think I can handle it?" Icicles hung from her stare.

He raised his hands. "No, no, that's not what I meant."

"Uh huh," she deadpanned. "See you tomorrow, Ryan."

Shit, shit, shit. He'd have to handle her with kid gloves.

I'd like to handle her without gloves. Without clothes, even.

Jaw clenched, he swatted away that intrusive thought and got back to work.

Chapter Three

♥

Seething with angst, Lilo glared at the big, balloon-decked RV parked beside Salty Dog's patio. As soon as this happy retirement/bon voyage party ended, that monster would carry her parents away, leaving her to face her new business partner with no fatherly cushion. Frankly, she'd rather chew broken glass.

She nursed an Irish Red Ale, her favorite among her dad's brews, and watched him exchange goodbye hugs with the Salty Dog crew and loyal customers.

Lilo blinked hard to banish threatening tears. She couldn't begrudge her parents their well-earned leisure time, but damn, she was going to miss them. Kind of embarrassing to be this torn up at her age. She'd had her own place since she was twenty, but Mom and Dad had always been nearby, giving Trappers Cove a homey, secure feeling. Without them, TC was just another confining small town.

Her friend Gemma Moore, who worked at her Aunt Zora's Psychic Emporium, sidled up and linked her arm with Lilo's. "Hard, isn't it?"

"Yeah." With a sigh, she rested her head on Gemma's shoulder. "They're good drivers, but I'll worry the whole time they're gone. Not to mention—" She gestured in Ryan's direction.

Gemma gave her a gentle smile. "I like Ryan. Overly polished, maybe, but beneath that cashmere sweater beats a good heart."

"Hmmph."

Arm in arm, they watched Dad cut his Happy Retirement cake, then open a huge pile of gifts. Lilo had already given them a portable propane fire pit and reclining camp chairs. Salty Dog's regular customers and staff gifted them all kinds of travel gear: Bungee cords, lanterns, stainless steel wine tumblers emblazoned with *On the Road Again*, goofy sun hats—everything the new nomads needed. A teary-eyed Quinn presented them with a hammock "for your well-earned naps." An equally soggy Wendy gave them a mini waffle maker. "Now, you make sure Olga gets a good breakfast, you hear?"

Marco and Mia's gift was a pair of fuzzy blankets printed with Salty Dog's logo—a muscular bulldog in sailor garb. Bringing up the rear, Ryan presented them with a pair of engraved beer steins and an assortment of beers, "So you won't get too homesick."

Lilo grumbled, "Sending Dad off with something he made. Tacky."

"Easy now." Gemma squeezed her arm. "I know you're hurting, but so is Ryan."

"Pssht. I'm sure he'd rather find a new brewer. He's just giving me a job out of obligation to Dad."

Gemma's sharp eyes peered right through Lilo's defenses. "How bad could it be? Ryan's a real sweetheart. After that terrible storm last month, he showed up every day until Jesse's greenhouses were rebuilt. A friend like that is hard to find."

This was news to Lilo. Her encounters with Ryan had all been framed by the brewery, where he struck her as a glib, glad-handing schmoozer. Difficult to put a finger on what bugged her so much—perhaps his phony smile that didn't quite reach his intense, dark eyes? He was undeniably handsome, with short, sandy hair and a chiseled chin, always impeccably dressed in expensive-looking sweaters that hugged his broad shoulders and slacks that molded to his long, muscular legs. But something about Ryan Lee triggered her defenses big time.

Eighth grade, dummy.

She shoved that thought into a mental strongbox and slammed the lid. There had to be more to this visceral distrust than that long-ago fiasco. Because who carries a grudge for twenty-five years? Certainly not a mature, level-headed woman like her.

"I don't trust him," she told Gemma. "When Dad dropped the bomb, Ryan just gave me this creepy, dead-eyed stare."

Gemma laughed. "Says the woman who could stare down an owl. His poker face is typical for a Capricorn." She nudged Lilo with her elbow. "You know, people often mistake Scorpios' intensity for coldness."

Lilo snorted. "Capricorn, huh? As long as Mr. Horny Goat Man stays out of my way, we'll get along fine. The brewery is my domain. Let him stick to the front of the house and flirt with the customers."

Gemma's eyes widened. "Aha. Jealous much?"

"Eew. I've known him since middle school. He's like an icky cousin I have to be nice to."

Gemma pecked her cheek and trotted across the patio to Jesse, her new boyfriend. She and the hunky herb farmer were an odd couple, but they seemed happy.

When a server passed with a tray of Pelican Pete's Pilsner, Lilo helped herself. She sipped and swished before swallowing. Very good for its class, but she craved something with more complexity. She'd assumed that when she started her own brewery, her dad would be around to bounce ideas off of, troubleshoot problems—but now he'd be in a camper in the Badlands of South Dakota or the swamps of Louisiana or some other god-forsaken place with shitty cell reception.

Not that she wasn't confident in her abilities. Between her travels through the Pacific Northwest and last year's tour of European breweries, she'd soaked up a ton of knowledge about beers she wanted to try, innovative ways to maximize output, and clever merchandising tricks. After fifteen years of helping other brewers perfect their products, she was finally ready to take her place as an innovator in the craft beer world.

But for the next year, her plans would sit on the shelf while she cranked out the same old same old—unless she could convince Ryan to loosen his grip on the beer menu.

Caught up in brooding, she jolted when warm arms encircled her from behind, carrying the sweet scent of honeysuckle.

"Oh, Punkin, we're going to miss you. I'm so glad you agreed to take over for your dad," Mom cooed. "You're more than ready. We both have faith in you."

Her eyes prickled, but she forced a note of cheer into her voice. "Thanks, Mom. I hope you have a wonderful time on the road. And keep an eye on Dad's lead foot."

After a long, clinging hug, Mom moved off to greet her poker buddies while Lilo pasted on a happy face and circulated until her cheeks hurt. Passing the firepit table, she glimpsed Ryan in close conversation with a pretty redhead. The woman giggled and tossed her hair.

Lilo's stomach twinged.

It's gonna be a looooong year.

Feeling a bit intrusive, Ryan watched Lilo say goodbye to Robert and Olga. Clearly, the steely eyed brew witch had a soft spot for her parents. Despite her brave smile, anyone with eyes could see she was hurting. And it was damn generous of her to take over for her dad on short notice, even if she was a grump-ass about it.

He'd hoped to enter Robert's beers in May's Rain Coast Brew Fest. The old guy was well respected in the Pacific Northwest brewing community, giving Salty Dog a fighting chance despite its small size. Would he have the same odds with a female brewer? A gorgeous one, to be sure, but the craft beer world was still rife with sexism.

With his arm around his sweet wife, Robert stepped to Ryan's side. "Well, it's time we hit the road."

Ryan's chest grew tight with emotion. This was it, the end of an era. He whistled for the crowd's attention.

"Thanks, everyone, for coming out to say goodbye to the best brewer ever to grace Trappers Cove. Robert, you are a gentleman, a beer scholar, a master of your craft, and—" his voice wobbled—"The best man I know. Bon voyage, my friend."

Robert squeezed him in a fierce hug, then faced the crowd. "My bride and I are ready to sail off into the sunset." He swiped his eyes with the back of his knuckly hand. "The Salty Dog crew has been like family to me. I'll miss you every day." He snugged his wife to his side. "But Olga tells me there's more to life than beer. Our first stop—one of those fancy spas in Napa. Might even try some wine." He wrinkled his nose, drawing a laugh.

While the crowd closed in for final goodbyes, Ryan withdrew to lean against the patio railing and compose himself. A moment later, Robert approached, towing Lilo by the arm. She didn't look too pleased about it.

"Son, you take good care of my little girl, you hear?"

Wincing, Lilo grumbled under her breath.

Ryan straightened and met Robert's gaze. "Yes, sir. I will."

"And Punkin, you keep an eye on this youngster. He doesn't know spit about brewing, but he's a good 'un all the same." He smooched her cheek, then he and Olga climbed into their RV and steered toward new adventure—and out of Ryan's life.

He and Lilo exchanged a long, stunned stare.

Awkward.

He cleared his throat and clasped his hands behind his back. "I'm looking forward to working with you, Lilo."

She scrunched her lips to the side. "We'll see."

Prickly woman. He'd have to win her over somehow. His livelihood depended on it.

Chapter Four

♥

The next day, Ryan watched Lilo through the glass, struck by her easy grace as she bent to fiddle with valves, stretched high to cinch a kettle hatch, and climbed the ladder to check her control panel. She tapped a finger against her plush lips, nodded, then hopped down, landing lightly as a cat. Really, he should just walk through the brewery door and wish her the best on her first day in charge. But that would mean the end of watching her captivating movements, and he wasn't ready to stop yet.

Lilo Eisinger was too damn attractive for his poor, stretched-taut brain to handle. Even in faded jeans and a flannel shirt, she radiated elegance and confidence. Her long ponytail swung with her quick motions, her expression relaxed and—happy? She certainly seemed at home among the mash tuns and kettles.

Tall, gangly Marco handed her a clipboard. She glanced at it, smiled, and clapped his shoulder. With a grin, he headed for the cold storage room in the back.

Ryan sighed and shook his head. At least Lilo got along with the brew crew, even if she didn't like him much. She probably sensed his inappropriate attraction. Why couldn't she look more like her jowly dad and less like her pretty, sharp-eyed mother?

As if reading his thoughts, Lilo glanced up and caught him staring. Her gaze held a note of challenge.

Might as well get started hashing out their working relationship. The longer he waited, the more awkward it would be.

Striding into the brewery, he rubbed his palms together. "So. Here we are, Lilo. First day of a new era."

She snorted. "I promised Dad a year, not an era."

"You don't intend to stay on?"

"Nope." She turned her attention to her clipboard.

Heat flushed his face, but he forced a mask of nonchalance and rocked back on his heels, pondering his next move. "Well, that's good to know. So I can plan. For the future." *Without your cantankerous ass.*

"Uh-huh. Gotta have a plan." As she climbed to the top of the mash kettle, he couldn't help noticing how beautifully her jeans cupped the curve of her derriere.

"Speaking of plans," she called from on high, "We're gonna need a new pump. If this old geezer dies, your whole brew house goes down."

Ryan raked his fingers through his hair. "First day in charge and you're already costing me money."

"Relax. I'll shop around, find you the best price." She gave him a sharp-toothed grin. "I've got connections."

"How come Robert never mentioned these things?"

She kept her back to him as she tinkered with tubing up there. "Dad believes in patching things up until they can't be revived anymore. Won't surprise me if he and Mom limp back into town with their RV held together by bubble gum and duct tape. Is that how you want to run your brewery?"

He kept his voice level, refusing to rise to her bait. "Shoot me a quote when you find the one you want. Speaking of plans, I was hoping to enter the Rain Coast Brew Fest this year. You've heard of it?"

She raised one eyebrow in a look of supreme snark. "Duh."

His jaw tightened. Lilo might have grown into a beautiful woman, but deep down, she was still the same snotty girl he'd known since middle school. It would be so satisfying to give her a verbal smackdown, but for the brewery's sake, he needed to rein in his temper.

"Thing is," he continued, "the master brewer has to be present."

"Right." Her eyebrow rose another centimeter.

"Would you consider it?"

Still on the ladder, she folded her arms and gazed down at him. "On one condition."

"And that would be...?"

"I pick the beers."

His face burst into flame. "Now just a hot minute, Lilo. I'm your boss."

"Are you now?" She lifted the hatch to peer inside the kettle. "Dad never called you his boss."

"That's different."

"How?"

"He has... uh... experience."

He felt his 'nads shrink under her withering glare. "Dad taught me everything he knows. You won't find another brewer as qualified as me."

"Pretty arrogant, aren't you?

Lilo shrugged. "I know my worth. And unlike my dad, I'm not content to stick with the status quo." She hopped down and faced him with her hip cocked. "I'm ambitious."

He drew up to his full height. "So am I."

A dazzling smile stretched Lilo's lips. "Good. You wanna put this place on the map? Let me try some new recipes."

"Like what?"

"For starters, a Belgian-style Kriek Lambic made with Rainier cherries."

Great. She's one of those beer snob weirdos.

"Listen, this isn't Portland or Seattle. Folks here want solid quality. Our IPA and Amber sell out every month. We need more of those beers, not fruity-patootie brews no one's ever heard of."

Her nostrils flared. "You won't win that competition with a boring IPA or Amber, no matter how much the locals like it with their fish and chips."

"Boring?" His voice rose to a rusty squeak. "Listen, Ms. Snooty Pants, I'm the captain of this ship. Your dad was my chief engineer, and that's your job now."

Why was her smirk so damn sexy? She stepped closer, right into his personal space. "Oh, I'm supposed to be your Scotty? You handle all the decisions, and I crank up production to Warp Five?" She slapped the tank behind her. "Let me tell you something, Cap'n. You want to increase production, you're going to need a bigger facility. In the meantime, your best chance to make your mark on the beer scene is to try something new."

They glared at each other for what felt like hours. Finally, he huffed. "I'll think about it."

"You do that." She flashed him a toothy smile, then returned to her work.

Ryan stomped back to his office, grumbling all the way. The nerve of her, thinking she was his partner! The bar and brewery were thriving under his leadership. No way was he going to turn over control to a cocky newcomer.

He slammed his office door and attacked a pile of invoices on his desk, ripping the envelopes into tiny shreds.

An unwelcome thought intruded. His mom had handled everything on her own for years after losing Dad. It wasn't until she retired from her job as high school secretary that he realized how exhausted she'd always been. Nowadays, pushing forty, he glimpsed her baggy-eyed, slump-shouldered appearance in his own reflection.

Having a partner to manage an expansion site would be such a relief. But if he took one on, it damn sure wouldn't be bossy-ass Lilo Eisinger, with her sultry gray gaze and sexy, growly voice, and...

He adjusted his suddenly too-tight pants. "Shut up, dick. You get no say in this."

Chapter Five

♥

Finally finished with her first shift, Lilo adjourned to the bar for a celebratory drink and one of Wendy's succulent salmon burgers.

Quinn looked up from muddling limes and mint, doffed her Trilby, and shouted, "Good people of Trappers Cove, meet your new head brewer!" Cheers and applause broke out.

Tickled, Lilo took a bow before climbing onto her bar stool. "Irish Red please, barkeep."

Quinn deposited her order with a flirtatious waggle of her pierced eyebrows. "Your beverage, my lady."

A moment later, Wendy personally delivered Lilo's sandwich. The guy seated next to her, a good-looking forty-something with long dreadlocks and a sexy smile, chatted her up as she wolfed down her dinner.

Quinn interrupted their banter. "Here comes the boss," she muttered out of the corner of her mouth as she scrubbed an imaginary spot on the bar.

Lilo sucked in a breath and braced herself for Ryan's brilliant smile—but he'd turned down the volume this evening. He propped his elbow on the bar and raised his chin in greeting. "Evening, Calvin. Lilo, how was your first day?"

"Not too bad." She licked sauce from her fingers, then pulled out her phone. "I'm making a list of repairs and upgrades."

His bland expression faltered for a nanosecond.

"Quality costs, Ryan. You should know that."

A muscle jumped in his jaw. "Would you excuse us, Calvin?"

With a shrug, her seatmate drained his beer and strolled over to the dartboards. Ryan took his seat. At long last, he dropped his mask and hissed through clenched jaws, "Why are you being so goddamn antagonistic?"

She couldn't quite rein in her grin. "Finally, the man speaks his truth. Wondered if you'd ever drop that poker face."

The furrow between his golden eyebrows deepened. "Other than honoring your dad's wishes and giving you a well-paid, full-time job, what have I done to piss you off?"

Let's start with the eighth-grade science fair.

Her conscience smacked her upside the head. *Really? Still chewing on that? Let it go.* She and Ryan were coworkers now—high time for a fresh start.

She dropped the smirk. "I'm just frustrated because I'm stuck."

"Well, I didn't stick you here. It was your dad who decided to retire." He pinched the bridge of his nose and gentled his voice. "I miss him like hell, by the way. And I want to keep what he built running smoothly. I owe him that."

Touched by his seeming sincerity, Lilo dropped her shield. "Yeah, I owe him too. He's given me the kind of education you can't get in brewing school. But paying him back means staying somewhere I don't want to be."

Ryan's gaze fell, then rose to meet hers again. Strange that a blond guy would have such deep brown irises, warm and shimmering and—

"Is being around me really so awful?"

Her head jerked backward at the raw hurt in his voice. Immediately contrite, she reached for his hand on the bar. "I'm sorry if I gave you that impression." A true statement—she could be blunt at times, but she didn't enjoy inflicting pain. "Dad was happy working here." Another true statement. "But I have bigger dreams, and I can't accomplish them in this cramped little brewery."

Ryan squeezed her hand, his grip warm and firm. "Well, so do I. What makes you think otherwise?"

She squirmed on her stool. "I guess you seem kind of—I dunno—smug?"

He jerked his hand away. "Look, am I proud of what I've accomplished here? Damn straight. Am I gonna sit on my laurels for the rest of my life? No way."

Interesting. She'd never considered that angle.

"Well, maybe if we walk on parallel paths for the next year, we can help each other move on to bigger and better things."

He gripped her shoulder, his touch setting off a cascade of shivers. "Lilo, we're not on parallel paths. We're on the same path. The Salty Dog path. I need your help, and you need mine." The corners of his lips twitched. "Or do you already have a big stash of start-up capital and a brewery site of your own?"

She huffed a strand of hair from her forehead. "Not exactly." The investment her dad promised was a year away. "But the way you're always checking on me pisses me off. Feels like you don't trust me."

Ryan straightened on his stool. "That wasn't my intention. You're just—"

She crossed her arms and waited.

"Look, Lilo. I really want to make this work out between us. Is that possible?"

Well, she did like challenges. Thrived on them, as a matter of fact. "Tell you what, I'll agree to a cease-fire if—"

Grinning, he seized her hand. "I knew you'd see reason."

Well, that's irritating. So was her enjoyment of his skin against hers.

"I said *if* you treat me with the same respect you gave my father."

"Deal." He shook her hand, squeezing firmly and holding her gaze—a challenge, or an invitation?

Her breath hitched—not from his iron grip, but from the intensity of his stare, those warm brown eyes a woman could fall into...

Shut up, libido.

"Well, I'd better get home." Reluctantly, she released his hand and slid to her feet. As she walked away, she felt his gaze burning into her back.

"Lilo, wait." Ryan trotted toward her, clutching a handful of T-shirts. "You're about Quinn's size, right?"

"Yeah. Why?"

"What's your favorite color?"

"Red."

He handed her a scarlet Salty Dog T-shirt. "To wear at work—I mean, if you want to." He twisted the toe of his shiny loafer on the tile floor. "Welcome to the family."

Aww. She clutched the shirt to her chest and wrestled her grin into submission. "Thanks, Ryan."

"Are you free tomorrow morning, say nine o'clock?"

"Um... sure?"

"Great. Let's meet at Cassie's Café to discuss our plans for Salty Dog." He shuffled a step closer and lowered his voice—and his thick, glossy lashes. What a killer combination. "A little strategizing over pancakes?"

Chuckling, she nodded. "Okay. It's a date."

He held up his forefinger. "It's a business meeting between col-leagues."

"Sure. Whatever. Cassie's at nine." Grinning, she pivoted and sashayed to the back door, putting a little extra swing in her step.

He likes me.

Chapter Six

♥

Lilo's running shoes slapped the packed sand at the shoreline. Her breath sawed in and out in counterpoint to the sliding surf. She'd already passed her usual three-mile mark, yet her pre-meeting nerves persisted. If she couldn't run them off, maybe she could shower them off. Up ahead, she spotted Salty Dog, the little upstairs balcony with its potted palm visible through the morning fog. Might as well use the five-minute walk home as her cool-down.

Stupid to be so jittery. It was only a breakfast meeting to discuss business plans—Ryan had made that abundantly clear. Not that she wanted a more personal connection. So what if his gaze gave her tummy flutters? Just a normal reaction in a healthy woman who'd been without sex for too long.

She jogged to a stop and propped her hands on her knees, her ribs squeezing like bellows. She loved the morning stillness, unlike in summer when families clogged the shoreline with their galumphing dogs, heedless little kids, and beach gear strewn everywhere. This morning, a light fog muffled traffic noise and cooled her flushed skin. Except for a few fishermen, she had the beach to herself. Scanning the horizon, she spotted a shiny black head bobbing in the surf. A seal? No, too much splashing. Definitely a person—a crazy one to be swimming in that icy water.

Transfixed, she watched the swimmer paddle toward shore and rise from the sea, encased in a black wetsuit. Broad shoulders, slim, muscular body, strong legs. Yum. He halted in knee-deep surf and gawked at her. Probably thought he had the beach to himself, just like she had.

"I'm impressed," she called. "Must take dedication to swim when it's this cold."

With a deep, sexy laugh, he pulled off his neoprene cap and goggles to reveal squashed blond hair and dancing dark eyes. "A compliment from Lilo Eisinger? Never thought I'd see the day."

Holy shit, it's Ryan. She flapped her hands with all the grace of a landed penguin. "I, uh, wanted to get in a run before our meeting."

He strode toward her, dripping as he tugged the zipper pull on the back of his wetsuit. "I get it. Hard exercise clears the mind."

Mesmerized, she watched his bare toes wiggle in the sand. Seeing him without his snazzy armor gave her all kinds of warm, fuzzy feelings. How embarrassing.

She jerked her gaze up to find him scanning her from head to toe and back. Thank God she'd worn her new running tights and not her raggedy old sweats. "Ocean swim in March. That's pretty badass."

He bowed with a flourish. "Why, thank you. Well, I'd better rinse off the salt before our breakfast. See you at nine." And off he went, slogging through soft sand toward the Salty Dog building. The flash of pale skin through his open zipper did funny things to her core.

"Wait, you're going to shower at the brewery?"

He turned back. "Don't worry, I won't get sand in your kettles. I live above the taproom. Didn't you know that?"

"No, I didn't. Must be nice, having such a short commute."

He lifted a shoulder. "You could say the same."

"You know where I live?" She wasn't sure if she liked that news or found it a little creepy.

Ryan rolled his eyes. "It's part of your payroll info. I know your birthday, too, Miss Scorpio." Grinning, he backed away, "I'd better stay out of range of your sting." He patted his very fine ass as he strolled toward Salty Dog, laughter rolling behind him.

Painfully good-looking and with a sense of humor—Ryan Lee was a huge distraction from her goals. She broke into a jog and headed for home to clean up. To get what she wanted out of this meeting, she'd need to bring her A game.

The best window table at Cassie's Coastal Café opened up just in time. Ryan plopped into a seat beneath a macrame planter of Devil's Ivy. The morning fog had cleared, and Aunt Cassie's kitschy stained-glass pelicans, unicorns, and mermaids glittered in the brilliant sunshine. The unusually fine weather brought people outdoors—in fact, the whole town seemed to be parading by. Just as well. The recollection of that guy flirting with Lilo last night still rankled. Not that he was planning to date his new brewer, but he didn't mind the idea of people seeing them together. Didn't mind at all.

She came striding up the street, her long dark hair flying like a satin flag. Despite her casual work outfit of snug jeans, running shoes, and a flannel shirt, she moved with impressive poise. The breeze blew her flannel open to reveal her new Salty Dog T-shirt beneath. *Nice.*

Coming from the opposite direction, Jesse and Gemma carried cartons of fresh herbs, probably bound for the food co-op. They greeted

Lilo, who gestured toward the café's window. Gemma flashed a wide grin, and Jesse gave a thumbs-up.

Since Lilo's return to Trappers Cove, Jesse kept dropping pointed comments about her overall hotness and suitability for a beer geek like him. Which was absurd, because he was a businessman. Lilo was the beer geek. The prettiest beer geek he'd ever met, but still.

He rose to get her attention. She waved, then nodded and smiled in response to whatever nonsense Jesse was spouting. The three of them threw their heads back and roared with laughter loud enough to hear through the glass.

Note to self: remind Jesse to mind his own fuckin' business.

Lilo pulled the café door open, and Cassie scooted around the counter to intercept her, waving jazz hands above her head like an ageing chorus girl. "Lorelei, how you doin', hon?" she squealed. "C'mere. Let me look at you."

With a sigh, Ryan sank back into his seat. By the time the whole town finished greeting Lilo, they'd have to take their breakfast to go. So much for a relaxed meeting on neutral ground.

Fussing and clucking, Cassie towed Lilo to their table and pushed her into a seat. "So, the two of you are together now. How nice." She clasped her hands over her heart and beamed.

"We're working together," he corrected his aunt. "And we'd like some breakfast before work, if you have time."

"Keep your pants on, buster." She lifted her order pad and addressed Lilo. "You want frittata or pancakes? Or both?"

"Frittata, please, with fruit and a side of bacon."

"That's my girl. How about you, kiddo?"

"Same, please."

Cassie finally left them after filling their coffee cups.

Ryan leaned onto his elbows. How to start this tricky negotiation? Best to ease into it. "So, why Lilo?"

She looked up from doctoring her coffee with cream and sweetener. "Why what?"

"How did Lorelei turn into Lilo? Shouldn't it be Loli?"

"Ah." She sipped, then added more sweetener. "Couldn't pronounce my name when I was little. I called myself Lilo, and it stuck."

Apparently, she'd reached the perfect sweetener overload, because she set her mug down and leaned onto her elbows, leveling him with the full force of her storm cloud gaze. Like electromagnets, those eyes—the big industrial kind that hoisted crushed cars. Once she aimed their power at you, it was impossible to look away.

"Why a brewery?" she asked.

"Pardon?"

"It's not an easy business to run. Tons of competition."

"Ah." Stalling, he gave his black coffee an unnecessary stir. How much detail to surrender?

"I grew up working in Cassie's kitchen while other kids were playing sports. Or, ya know, drama." He pressed his wrist to his forehead in a theatrical gesture.

Lilo arched an eyebrow. "Let's get this on the table. I didn't like you back then. You didn't like me either. We're grownups now. Let's move on."

Huh? Move on from what? He and Lilo were in the same graduating class but never interacted much. He remembered her as scary-sexy, slinking through the school halls on chunky Doc Martens, glaring at him through black-rimmed eyes. If she'd addressed him directly, he'd have pissed himself in terror.

He cleared his throat and reminded himself he was no longer that dorky, awkward kid. "In college, I used to hang out at this old-school bar in Pullman—a fun, friendly dive. The Swizzle Stick, it was called. Everyone knew everyone there, like that old TV show. But it was a mess, and I filled my notebooks with ideas to polish up the place. So when I came back to Trappers Cove and saw the For Sale sign in Salty Dog's window, that was it, my chance to manifest everything I'd daydreamed about during all those boring business classes at WSU."

Lilo nodded, her gaze dreamy. "Yeah, I know just what you mean."

"It took a ton of work and some dicey financing to shape her into the kind of place I'd always wanted to run—classy but casual, hip but welcoming. Not like those uber-trendy nightspots in Portland or Seattle where you've gotta prove you're cool enough to buy an overpriced drink."

Lilo wrinkled her nose. "Snobs suck."

Even beer snobs? He wisely kept that thought to himself.

Lilo leaned closer, her gaze sharp and probing. "But you want more."

For a heart-stopping moment, he thought she meant...

She arched an eyebrow. "You're looking to expand?"

At once relieved and oddly disappointed, he nodded. "I figure, why not take what I've learned and establish a string of Salty Dogs? The trick is finding the right combination of location, charm, and potential for growth—like here in TC, where the summer crowds give me a booster shot of cash." He was talking too much and too fast, but if anyone sympathized with his ambitions, it would be Lilo. "But I don't ever want to be one of those business owners who boards up for the off season. I want to contribute to the community, you know?"

She tilted her head and gave him a long, cool gaze. Uncomfortably long. Thank God a server arrived with their food.

He took a bite of cheesy, spicy, veggie- and sausage-filled frittata. "How about you?"

"What about me?"

"Why beer?"

She speared a chunk of melon and shrugged. "I like beer, and I like a challenge. I grew up tinkering with Dad's home brews." She dropped her gaze and gave an endearing, crooked grin. "I used to feel like a mad scientist in a lab. Anyway, I want to expand on his legacy. It's a male-dominated field, so—" She lifted one shoulder. "A woman's gotta be twice as good as her male competitors to get noticed."

"And you're twice as good?"

Holding his gaze, she popped the fruit into her mouth. How did she make chewing look so damn seductive? "Yeah, I am." Her grin widened. "Maybe more."

I'll bet you are. No way he was just imagining the flash of heat in her stare.

After demolishing his food, he smacked his palms together. "So, let's have it."

She fumbled her fork. "Have what?"

"Your ambitions. What beers do you want to add to our list? Besides the cherry one." Which sounded freakin' weird, but in the spirit of teamwork, he'd listen and keep his reactions to himself.

"I'd like to try some European classics—Flemish Red or Berliner Weisse."

Ryan gave a low whistle to cover his ignorance. "How are you gonna do that in such a small facility?"

"Easy. We dedicate one brew kettle to a monthly special. Offer different beers. Scarcity marketing. When it's gone, it's gone, so that's an incentive to come in more often."

He hadn't expected a brewer to sling business terms with such ease. "Beautiful and smart."

She scowled. "Don't try to distract me with flattery. Then we do market analysis, see which ones are most popular."

Damn. His flirty banter usually got a warmer reception. "Who says I'm trying to distract you?"

Lilo leaned back in her chair and crossed her arms. "You're pretty transparent with your phony smile and your bedroom eyes. You and I are stuck together professionally. Let's make the best of it and not muddy the waters with flirtation."

"There's that Scorpio sting Gemma warned me about."

"Gemma warned you about me?" Judging by Lilo's sour expression, Gemma was due for a talking to.

"She and Jesse stopped by yesterday. She says Scorpios are like coconuts. Hard, scratchy exterior, soft and juicy interior. According to her, Capricorn and Scorpio have a lot in common. She says, with my practicality and your intuition, we'd make a great team."

Lilo's eyes narrowed. "What kind of team do you have in mind?"

"I'm talking about work, of course. Although—" He stroked his chin, weighing his chances. "I wouldn't object to getting to know you better. On a personal level."

Her eyebrows rose, then scrunched. She licked her lips, then clamped them tight. What the hell was going on in that hard head of hers?

Finally, she set down her fork and folded her hands on the table. "I'm gonna be straight with you, Ryan. I'm attracted to you."

Yesss! He schooled his features into a blasé expression. "Is that so?"

"But I'm not the casual hookup type. I have to at least like a guy before getting intimate. And I'm not sure I like you."

His jaw fell. "What the hell did I do?"

She gave a slow, feline blink. "Besides being a schmoozer who doesn't have faith in my skills as a brewer?"

"I never said— "

"Your actions say otherwise, always watching me to make sure I don't screw up."

Time to meet boldness with boldness. "Did it ever occur to you I just like looking at you?"

Her eyes flashed as she scraped back her chair. "Is that why you asked me here? To butter me up, then hit on me?"

"No, I— "

She stabbed a finger toward his chest. "Gemma didn't finish her lesson on Scorpios. She didn't tell you we hate feeling manipulated." She crumpled her napkin, threw it onto her plate, and tossed a wad of bills onto the table.

He pushed to his feet. "For fuck's sake, Lilo."

The room went silent. He felt the prickly weight of two dozen stares.

Shit on a flaming stick.

He lowered his voice. "Look, I'm sorry I didn't do backflips when Robert told me you were taking over. I was in shock, okay?"

She blew out a long breath and dropped her gaze to her lap. "Me too."

He sat again and leaned toward her, smearing his sleeve with jelly. "Please, Lilo, explain what I did to make you so dead set against me?"

Her eyebrows inched upward. "You really don't remember, do you? The eighth-grade science fair?"

He shrugged, completely at sea.

She gripped the edge of the table, her knuckles white, her words tumbling fast and furious. "I spent a month on that fermentation project. Right before the judges got to my display, you and your chucklehead buddies ran up and chugged all my samples. Then you,

Ryan Edward Lee, puked all over my table. A month of preparation, gone."

Ryan felt the blood drain from his face when the memory swam into focus. As the new kid in school, he was desperate for friends, and he found them in a bunch of numbnuts who pulled stupid stunts.

He swiped a hand down his face. "I'm so sorry, Lilo. I'd forgotten about that. If it's any consolation, I got suspended for a week, and everyone called me Captain Puke for the rest of the year."

She crossed her arms and glowered.

"My mom grounded me for a month. I missed the Sadie Hawkins dance." He summoned his sincerest smile. "Maybe if I hadn't been such an asshole, you and I could have been friends."

He extended his hand, a peace offering. She stared at it as if he'd plopped a jellyfish onto the table.

There had to be a way to get through to her. His lips quirked upward as an idea flickered to life.

"Tell you what—you want that blue ribbon? Let's see that you win it. At the Rain Coast Brew Fest."

She smirked. "Pretty slick. That's what you wanted all along."

"It's not all I want, but you obviously don't return my feelings, so I'll settle for this."

"And claim the glory for yourself."

He threw up his hands. "Don't be such a hard-ass, Lilo. I'm not a pubescent chucklehead anymore. I'm your business partner."

Her smile bloomed slow and venomous. "Okay, partner. Let's talk beers."

Aargh! She got me. Just like that, he'd gone from boss to equal. *Skillfully played, Lilo.*

Chapter Seven

❤

Lilo marched up Main Street, past souvenir shops, art galleries, and T-shirt vendors. When she reached Madame Zora's Psychic Emporium, she flung open the door and stormed inside.

The shop's namesake looked up from dusting fairy figurines and flashed a warm, motherly smile. "Hello, Lorelei. Looking for Gemma?" She smoothed her batik tunic over her ample hips. "Or are you here for a reading?"

The only thing Lilo was interested in reading was the bumps she was going to give her friend's head for encouraging Ryan's romantic ambitions.

"She's finishing up with a palmistry client. I'll get you a tea while you wait." The older woman bustled to her antique samovar and filled a mug. "You'll love this blend. Rose hips and sweet spices. Now that Gemma and Jesse are paired up, he's sharing his grandmother's recipes." She winked. "Nice bonus, eh? So, I hear you're taking over at Salty Dog."

"Yes, ma'am. For a while, anyway."

"I'll have to stop by and try your wares. And one of Wendy's fish sandwiches." She gave a belly-shaking chuckle that made her dangly earrings tinkle.

Gemma emerged from behind the carved wooden screen, followed by Mo Abadi, proprietor of Ali Baba's Kebabs. Mo's bushy eyebrows drew together. "I'll think about that. You may be right." He caught Lilo's eye. "Well, hello there. How are Robert and Olga doing? Thursday night poker's not the same without them."

"So far, so good." Mom had sent a flurry of photos that morning—her and Dad posed with hay-bale sculptures, a giant concrete artichoke, and a wooden yeti carved with a chainsaw. Every snap displayed her parents' huge grins. They were having the time of their lives.

After Mo left, Gemma pulled Lilo behind the screen. Eyes bright, she bounced on her toes. "How's it going with Ryan? I think he's into you."

"Thanks to you. Why'd you put that idea in his head?"

Gemma backed away, palms out. "Hey now, I didn't plant any seeds. His eyes light up like sparklers whenever he mentions you. I merely warned him what he was up against."

Lilo huffed. "I don't need that kind of energy between Ryan and me. I'm stuck with him for a whole effin' year, and I want to make this connection an opportunity, not a roadblock."

"How is his liking you a roadblock?"

Arms crossed, Lilo paced the tiny space. "It muddies the waters, clouds my thinking."

Gemma tapped her lips and dashed to the crystal display. "Hang on." She returned with a polished black stone, which she pressed into Lilo's palm. "Obsidian. Good for keeping your mind and heart clear."

Lilo's stiff shoulders relaxed as she hugged her friend. "Thanks, Gem. Sorry for barking at you. Something about that guy riles me up."

Gemma fiddled with the enameled pins holding her long, tawny hair. "Still that middle school deal? Isn't it time to let that go?"

"It's not just that. I don't like the way he stares at me. It makes me itchy."

Gemma chuckled. "Itchy or horny?"

"Okay, okay. His hotness is distracting."

Still laughing, Gemma pointed to the low table behind the screen. "Sit."

With an exasperated sigh, Lilo complied.

Gemma pulled out a deck of tarot cards. "Aunt Zora's been coaching me. Let's see what the cards say."

Lilo huffed. "You know I don't believe in that stuff."

"Humor me." She handed the deck to Lilo. "Close your eyes and breathe. Focus on your question."

"What question?"

"What to do about your attraction to Ryan, obvs."

Jaw tight, Lilo forced steady breaths and concentrated on Ryan Lee's maddening grin, his razor-sharp jaw, his mocking dark eyes, his lithe body emerging from the surf like some ancient sea god...

Gemma's low voice soothed her frazzled nerves. "Shuffle until your intuition tells you it's time to stop."

Sure enough, Lilo felt an undeniable nudge as the cards slipped through her hands. She laid them on the table. "Okay."

"Now pick a card. Top, middle, bottom of the deck, whatever feels right."

Eyes closed, Lilo chose one, then opened her eyes. "The fool? Perfect."

Gemma grinned. "Actually, it is. Upright like this, the fool symbolizes new ventures." She tapped the card. "This little fool is a reminder to open your open mind and your heart. Trust the path you're on and see where it leads."

"You need more tarot lessons," Lilo grumbled.

Gemma threw back her head and laughed. "You still on for girls' night? Dani's cooking. Her Frenchie chicken is to die for. Come over after your shift at the brewery."

"Yeah, okay. Thanks." She hugged her friend and left, pondering as she walked up Main Street toward Salty Dog. Maybe it was time to be honest with herself—she wanted Ryan. Like, a lot. And this snarl of emotion and lust wouldn't unknot until she relaxed her tight control.

He'd apologized, after all. Would it hurt to give him a chance to prove he'd changed?

Ryan paused his morning ocean swim to tread water and search the shore. He'd set his towel and gym bag close to Lilo's place, hoping to spot her running on the beach again, but for the past three days there'd been no sign of her. She was definitely avoiding him.

After their breakfast at Cassie's café, he'd stuck to his word and checked on her less often, which was damned difficult considering how the plate glass separating the brewery from the bar put her every movement on display. Her easy grace made the brewing process look like a dance.

Yesterday, he turned around and caught her watching him. "Shoe's on the other foot now," his mom would say. But Lilo was still as prickly as ever. Had he imagined the part where she admitted she was attracted to him?

A rogue wave doused him, yanking his thoughts back to the present. After a final lap, he swam for shore. The burn in his muscles felt good, cleansing even, and more effective than a cold shower for his simmering sexual frustration.

In the distance, a runner approached in red running tights and a bright yellow windbreaker, a cap jammed low over her eyes, her dark ponytail swinging with each step.

"Lilo, hey." Waving like an overenthusiastic dork, he splashed toward the waterline.

She stumbled to a stop, shielded her eyes, and peered out to sea. Then she doffed her cap, unzipped her jacket, and wiped her sweaty face with her T-shirt, baring a swath of smooth, pale belly. The curve from her waist to her hip was mesmerizing.

Ryan peeled off his cap and goggles, and pulled the zipper tab on his wetsuit. The cool wind was delicious on his sweaty skin. So was Lilo's intent gaze.

Normally he'd peel off his wetsuit and change into dry clothes, but what if she took that as a come-on? On the other hand, the friction from walking home in a wetsuit would leave him with a wicked rash.

He dug his icy toes into the sun-warmed sand and patted his chest. "You mind if I shuck this?"

Her eyes widened. "Go ahead."

Turning away, he quickly pulled off the suit, toweled himself dry, and pulled a hoodie over his bare torso. "Haven't seen you on the beach lately."

Her gaze slid down and to the side. "I've been running in town."

Yup, she's avoiding me. Don't push.

"How far do you run?" He turned back to find her chewing her lip, her face firetruck red.

"Two, three miles. Depends how I feel."

Damn, she wasn't making this easy.

"Gonna run some more?"

"Nah." Reaching behind her, she grabbed her foot with both hands and lifted it to her butt. "Why'd you start your swim so close to my place?"

"Oh, is your place near here?"

She dropped her foot and swatted his arm. "Cut the crap." She sank into a deep lunge, and he nearly swallowed his tongue.

He sat on his towel and pulled his gym bag over his lap to cover the evidence of his arousal. "Gorgeous day, right? I love being out here while the beach is still quiet." He pointed to a passing formation of pelicans skimming low over the water. "Just you, me, and the squadron."

She sank down beside him with a sigh. "Yeah, it's peaceful."

A fat seagull tap-danced toward them, ruffling its wings.

Ryan checked his bag. "Sorry, bud. Got nothing for you."

Lilo pulled a half-eaten granola bar from her pocket, broke off a chunk, and tossed it to the bird. A dozen more landed.

"Now you've done it."

The flock attracted a damp, galumphing golden retriever who barreled toward them, then skidded to a stop, spraying them with sand. Lilo doubled over with a yelp.

He gripped her arm. "What's wrong?"

"Sand in my eye."

"Here." He grabbed his water bottle and held her hair while she rinsed her eye.

"Better, but it still hurts." She pushed to her feet and stumbled over a piece of driftwood.

"Let me help." He tossed his things into his duffel, hefted it over his shoulder, and circled her waist with his arm, steering her around obstacles until they reached the shoreline road.

"That's me." She pointed to a blue-gray cottage with white trim.

He helped her up the stairs. Inside, instead of the kitschy nautical décor most folks in Trappers Cove adopted, he found sleek, modern furnishings in shades of ivory, gray, and plum. Very elegant. Very Lilo.

She stepped to the kitchen sink and rinsed her eye with the spray nozzle while he fetched towels to staunch the spreading puddles.

She plucked a towel from his hand. "You don't have to do that. I've got it from here."

"I'll stick around to make sure you don't need a ride to the clinic."

"If you insist." She straightened and patted her eye gingerly. "How's it look?"

Cupping her cheek, he turned her head toward the light and leaned in close, inches from her stormy gray eyes. She softly grasped his arm. Her breath fanned over his skin. Her lips parted. The air between them thickened like honey, golden and sweet and heavy with promise. Heart thundering, he waited.

She sucked in a breath and drew back.

Damn. "Your eye's a little red. Can you see okay?"

"Yeah. No permanent damage." Her smile was sheepish, her cheeks flaming pink. "Thanks for your help. See you at work."

Shot down in flames. No, ice. He trudged toward the door, then turned back. "So, we're just gonna ignore that?"

She blinked rapidly and clutched the towel over her heart. "Ignore what?"

"That moment we just shared."

Her gaze slid away, her usual bravado gone.

Frustrated, he sliced a hand through the distance between them. "Don't tell me you didn't feel it."

"A wise woman doesn't act on every passing notion," she grumbled.

Disappointment weighted his shoulders. "I get it. You still don't like me."

She glanced at him, then away, then back again. "That's not exactly true. But liking my business partner too much is dangerous for both of us. We should focus on our mutual goal—growing Salty Dog into a brewing empire, right?"

"Empire?" He snorted. "Maybe I have a different goal." Unwilling to give up hope, he moved closer and brushed a strand of hair from her damp cheek. "Seems stupid to pass up an opportunity when all signs are pointing to a big payoff."

Her mouth twisted in a wince. "Is that financial talk meant to be sexy? Am I supposed to come back with a crack about your bottom line?"

Chuckling, he raised his palms in surrender. "You know, I'm usually pretty good at flirty banter, but with you, everything I try falls flat. You've got some kind of anti-flirtation death ray."

Her gaze drifted downward again. "I can't help feeling defensive around you."

He reached for her hands and—hallelujah—she let him take them. "We're never going to build an empire if we're afraid of each other. Tell you what—you like a challenge, so I challenge you to endure a dinner with me at Francesca's. Call it a celebration of our partnership. I'll rein in my cheesy lines if you'll sheath your stinger. Deal?"

She chewed her lip. "Just dinner?"

"Scout's honor. I promise not to push for anything you don't want."

Her sigh could've extinguished a bonfire. "Okay. You win this round." She gave his shoulder a playful shove. "Now get your sandy feet off my floor."

"Right." He backed toward the door. "I'll see you at work. Take care, Lorelei."

Outside, bright sunshine painted everything in shiny, vibrant colors because Lilo had unlocked the door between them. He'd need to move with great care, but the light shining through that cracked door gave him hope. Grinning like the lucky bastard he was, he broke into a run as he headed toward home.

Chapter Eight

♥

Lilo checked her bedroom mirror and adjusted the neckline of her burgundy satin blouse to show just a little more cleavage. All day, she'd struggled to focus on work as her mind wandered again and again to tonight's dinner with Ryan—what to wear, what to talk about, and most of all, how their evening would end. A chaste kiss? A steamy one? More?

She hadn't worn this femme fatale outfit in quite a while. If nothing else came of this date, it was nice to have an occasion to pull out all the stops. Besides, dressing up made her feel powerful, and her towering heels would put her eye to eye with Ryan. She spritzed her décolletage with perfume, a spicy floral scent with hints of patchouli and sandalwood, then adjusted the jeweled clip holding her hair back on one side.

Kind of weird how deeply she cared about making a good impression tonight. Ryan was her coworker, after all—much more important to impress him with her brewing skills—but she couldn't help obsessing about how close she'd come to kissing him. The steamy memory blew her mind and dampened her panties. No doubt about it, she was battling for control against some powerful chemistry.

When the doorbell rang at seven on the dot, she gave herself a final inspection, straightened her posture, and strutted forth to greet her—*gulp*—date.

She flung open the door and nearly swallowed her tongue.

Ryan always dressed impeccably at Salty Dog, but tonight he'd gone above and beyond, wearing a long, sleek camel jacket over a black cashmere sweater that molded to his chest and set off his dark blond hair. Slim charcoal slacks hugged his powerful thighs, and his black ankle boots gleamed. He gripped a small package wrapped in the Sea Queen Spa's signature silvery paper.

Eyes bright, he drank her in from head to expensively shod toe, then he shoved his free hand through his hair, mussing the perfect waves. "I hardly recognized you. You look—different."

So much for her ego. She crossed her arms and gave him a cool stare. "I like to dress for the occasion. At work I dress like a brewer." She cocked a hip, causing the slit in her black leather midi skirt to fall open. "I'm not working tonight."

Ryan spluttered. "I meant you look amazing. Elegant. Dramatic." Bright spots of color stained his cheeks as he held out the gift.

That's better. She beckoned him inside and tore the wrapping paper to reveal a fat candle, deep red like her blouse and the accent pillows on her dove-gray sofa. Interesting—he'd noticed her favorite color. She sniffed—spicy notes that echoed her perfume. Impressive attention to detail.

"It's lovely. Thank you, Ryan. You clean up nice too." She tweaked his silk pocket square and inhaled his subtle cologne. "Moss, cedar, and pepper. That's very you. And a pinkie ring." She gave him a teasing smile. "Very fahncy."

His smile flattened. "It was my dad's."

Open mouth. Insert Manolos. "Was?"

He extended his fingers and gazed at the ring, a heavy silver piece emblazoned with an anchor. "Commercial fisherman. Lost at sea. You really didn't know?"

"Honestly, I didn't. I'm so sorry." She grasped his hand.

He let her hold it but didn't squeeze back. "That's why we came to TC. Cassie is my mom's sister. She put us up until Mom got back on her feet."

Guilt karate-kicked Lilo's ribs. How had she missed that crucial part of his history? He'd learned a lot about her family, thanks to his long association with Dad, but she didn't know diddly about his. And now she'd poked him right where it hurt most. "That must've been tough."

He shrugged, but his grim expression revealed the depth of his pain. "It was. New kid in town, widowed mom, on the free lunch program, bought our clothes from the thrift shop. Kids made fun because I came to school in their castoffs." He stroked his sweater. "Now that I can afford it, I like to splurge on the good stuff."

Giving in to temptation, she skated her fingers over the cloud-soft wool and the firm muscles beneath. "A self-made man. I admire that."

"At last, a compliment." The corners of his mouth ticked up. "Let's get going before my luck runs out."

She draped a knit wrap over her shoulders and followed him to his ginormous Ram pickup.

"Sorry for the climb." He flashed a sheepish grin as he opened the passenger door. "Want a boost?"

"I've got this." She planted a stiletto on the step bar, grabbed the handle, and swung herself up. Her skirt's slit gaped, baring her thigh.

Ryan made a sound somewhere between laughter and choking. "Is that what I think it is?"

She tugged her skirt aside to display her hops tattoo. "Like I said, brewing's in my blood."

"Talk about commitment to your craft."

"Damn straight." She gave him a cocky smile.

Planted below her, he held her gaze for a long, long time. Butterflies, fireflies, hummingbirds—all kinds of happy little creatures fluttered in her belly.

"How's your eye?" he asked at last.

"Oh, much better, thanks." She swallowed her disappointment at mistaking that lingering look for heat. What kind of game was he playing with her?

The old-school elegance of Casa Francesca hadn't changed. Perched on a cliff north of town, Trappers Cove's fanciest restaurant sat like an ageing Hollywood star bathed in the glow of hidden spotlights. While they waited in the marble-tiled lobby, Lilo drank in the glorious, mafia-movie décor—tufted red leather seats, gleaming dark paneling on the walls, Tiffany shades on the lamps. Potted palms between the tables gave the diners privacy. Servers in tuxedo shirts, scarlet cummerbunds, and black slacks bustled to and fro while an old dude with slicked-back hair tickled the ivories on a baby grand in the corner. In the rear, a glass wall revealed a panoramic view of the sea below.

The maître d', tucked two leather-bound menus under his arm. With his perfect posture, prominent nose, and salt-and-pepper hair, he reminded Lilo of Vincent Price. "Good evening, Mr. Lee, Ms. Eisinger. Right this way."

Ryan crooked his arm, suave as any romance novel hero. As they followed the host to their table, he whispered, "In Mom's bowling league, he's plain old Larry. But here, he's Lorenzo, all starched and proper."

Lilo bumped his hip with hers. "People have facets, Ryan. Like jewels."

Chalk it up to Ryan's schmoozing skills—Lorenzo seated them at a prized window table and beckoned to a server. "Aperitivo della casa," he purred as the she set down two champagne flutes of sparkling wine tinged with Campari. "Elizabeth will be your server this evening. Buon Appetito."

After perusing the mile-long menu, they ordered an antipasto platter to start. Lilo folded a paper-thin slice of prosciutto onto a golden crostino, took a bite, and closed her eyes in bliss. When she opened them, Ryan was watching her intently. Self-conscious, she brushed crumbs from her lips. "Ever think of offering something like this at the bar?"

He speared a chunk of marinated artichoke. "We do sometimes. Local cured meats, cheese from Oregon, olives from NorCal, pesto made from Ryan's herbs, bread from Garrett's bakery, and pickled Rainier cherries."

She tasted the butter-soft prosciutto and gave a tiny moan. "Speaking of cherries, my Kriek Lambic will be ready for tasting next week."

He pulled a face worthy of a six-year-old eating Brussels Sprouts.

"Come on, it's delicious, and it'll impress the hell out of the beer fest judges. It's an iconic brew."

Ryan's gaze dropped to his plate. "We'll decide which beers to enter in the competition when it's closer to the deadline."

His shifty body posture meant he had no intention of putting her Kriek in front of the judges. He'd change his mind once he tasted it.

He nudged the last marinated mushroom toward her. "What else have you got cooking?"

"Found a place in Oregon that offers smoked malt, so I'm experimenting with Smoked Porter and a Bamberger Rauchbier. Have you ever tried it?"

"Rau—what now?"

"I discovered it last summer in Germany. It's totally addictive." Caught up in the delicious memory, she leaned toward him. "See, until the 1800s, malt was toasted over an open fire. The wood smoke gives it a unique flavor. Really good with BBQ. I'll bet Wendy could—"

His hand fell over hers. "Hold on a minute. Wendy can get pretty touchy about her menu. How about you stick to beer, and *if* the customers like it, I'll deal with the kitchen, okay?"

She huffed a sigh. "Are you going to be this difficult all year?"

There it was again, that infuriating poker face. Why couldn't he just be straight with her?

He squeezed her hand. "Let's not argue over beers tonight. I want to get to know you better."

"All right." She forced her posture to relax. "What do you want to know?"

"You're, ah—" He chewed his lip. "You're single, right?"

"Of course." She narrowed her eyes. "I wouldn't be here if I weren't."

He squirmed in his seat. "It's just—some people like to keep their options open."

Her muscles tensed. Better to lay her terms on the table before she let her feelings cloud her judgment.

"Ryan, if there's going to be a second date, know this—I don't do the 'pick me' dance. When I date a guy, he gets my sole focus for however long we're together, and I expect the same from him."

His eyes widened for a split second before his suave mask slid back into place. He dabbed his tight lips with his napkin.

Pretty intense discussion for a first date, but he started it. She softened her tone and laid her hand over his tightly corded forearm. "Look, some people don't share food. I don't share lovers. If that doesn't work for you, we'll call this a business meeting. No hard feelings."

He held her gaze for a long, fraught moment. "I appreciate your honesty, Lilo." A crooked grin tilted his lips as his nervous fingers crumbled a piece of bread. "Anyone ever tell you you're intimidating?"

"Sure. But I'd rather be intimidating than be someone's plaything." No matter how strong their attraction, she knew her worth.

He covered her hand with his own. At his touch, warmth bloomed up her arm. "I'm not seeing anyone at the moment. My last girlfriend got a job offer in the Seattle area and—" He spread his fingers. "Poof, gone."

"That sucks. You deserve better treatment."

His grin widened. "How do you know?"

"We may not agree on what constitutes prize-winning beer, but that doesn't mean I don't appreciate your finer qualities."

"Like what?" His eyebrows inched higher.

Cool your jets, Mr. Flirty-Pants. "Like making sure an injured brewer gets home safe."

He laughed, a low, sexy rumble. "Well, the success of my business rests in my brewer's lovely hands." Her core temperature soared as he massaged her knuckles with slow arcs of his thumb.

Damn, this guy played a mean game of seduction. Keeping her wits about her was going to be tough.

He pushed his plate away. "So, you've heard a lot of my history tonight. Tell me all about the mysterious Lilo Eisinger."

She glanced over her shoulder, hoping for a reprieve. No sign of their server. "Well, you know the important stuff already—Dad, beer, I want my own brewery, blah, blah, blah."

He leaned back in his chair and laced his hands behind his head, causing his sweater to hug his chest and arms. "Don't be coy, Lilo. I told you about my love life. Your turn."

She swiped a chunk of bread through the olive oil on her plate. They were diving much deeper than she'd intended. If it were up to her, she'd never mention Tony at all, but fair is fair.

"I was briefly married in my early twenties. He wasn't a bad guy. We were just too young for that kind of commitment. Since then, there've been boyfriends, some serious, some not. It's hard to maintain a relationship when you travel as much as I have these past few years." Her smile felt brittle and false. "Good thing I enjoy my own company."

"It's nice to enjoy someone else's company, though." His smile bloomed slow and seductive. Reflected candlelight danced in his dark irises.

Breaking the spell, their server arrived with their meal, Osso Buco-style lamb shanks served with saffron risotto, the meat subtly spiced, succulent, and melt-in-your mouth tender. She licked her fork clean, raised her eyes to the heavens, and moaned.

Ryan leaned forward with a conspiratorial grin. "Isn't this the best? My friend Ben raises the lamb for this dish, and Jesse grows the herbs. Have you been out to his place?"

"Not yet. Gemma wants me to visit. Did you hear she's moving in with him? They've only known each other for—how long, a few months?"

"Yeah, that's a big step. But they seem to work well together." He set down his fork and tented his fingers. "We'll have to see how it goes this first year, but I've been thinking about partnering with you on a more permanent basis." He laid his hand over hers, his touch silky-soft, his expression earnest.

Panic sped her pulse and tightened her throat. Of course she'd wondered what it would be like to partner up with Ryan in a more personal way. In fact, she'd imagined it vividly. She tried for a glib answer, but all that emerged from her mouth was a harsh croak.

Ryan's shoulders slumped. "Wow, you still don't like me."

"That's not true," she hurried to assure him. "Your micro-managing is annoying, but I can defend my boundaries."

"I noticed." Chuckling, he nudged her knee with his. "Look, you want your own brewery, and I want to expand Salty Dog. Working together, we could accomplish great things and meet both our goals."

She giggled, embarrassed. "Oh. You weren't talking about a more personal kind of partnership."

He raised an eyebrow. "I didn't say that."

Fighting frustration, she twisted her napkin in her lap. "You're so damn hard to read, Ryan. If we're going to be partners, I need you to be straight with me."

He leveled a long, steady, impenetrable gaze. "Okay. I'm impressed with your work, and I'm very attracted to you. I'm hoping we can blend those two areas."

"You make it sound like some kind of corporate merger." Goose-bumps prickled her skin at the memory of yesterday's near kiss, his face so close to hers, the air between them thrumming with electricity.

Ryan rapped the table. "Hey, Ms. Be-Straight-With-Me, don't change the subject."

Why did this have to be so damn complicated? She pushed back her plate and folded her hands. "Ryan, when I leave Salty Dog, I'll become your competition."

"*If* you leave."

She narrowed her eyes. "Why can't I shake the feeling you just want me to make the brewery side of the business easy for you, like Dad did?"

"Hey, I'm willing to try your weird beers."

He countered her scowl by squeezing her hand. "Maybe we'll part ways down the road, but for now, I think we could make a great team if we can figure out how to keep from stepping on each other's toes."

Another flash of memory—his bare toes flexing in the sand. A hot flush climbed from her chest to her cheeks. She prayed the low lighting would hide her discomfort as fierce attraction warred with common sense. Closing her eyes, she waited for her inner wisdom to pronounce a verdict.

Nada. Perhaps that tarot card was right. Would it hurt to keep an open mind? Especially with such a tempting offer on the table. There was no denying her body's response to Ryan's flirty banter, his deep, velvety voice, his total focus on her reactions. This man was a skilled player in the game of seduction.

She straightened in her seat. "I'm not ready to commit yet, but I'm intrigued by the possibility."

His smile took on a playful glimmer. "In the beer sphere, or the personal sphere?"

"We'll see." She picked up her fork. "Now, let's enjoy this amazing meal before it gets cold."

An hour later, Ryan scooped up the last bite of tiramisù and held his fork to her mouth, a teasing grin on his too-damn-pretty face. "Come on, Lilo. Give in to temptation."

Oh, you want to play?

She gripped his wrist and wrapped her lips around the sweet morsel. "Mmm. Delicious." She licked her lips for good measure, then offered him the last bite of lavender-scented panna cotta. When custard drib-bled onto her hand, Ryan licked her skin clean.

Her panties nearly combusted.

With a discreet throat-clearing, Lorenzo stepped up to the table and asked if they cared for an espresso.

An innocuous question, but that jolt of after-dinner caffeine could signal the end of their increasingly heated encounter—or it could open the gate to something even hotter. And though her common sense shrilled like a referee's whistle, she regarded Ryan from beneath half-lowered lids. "I have an espresso machine at home. I could make us a caffè corretto."

After all, she could make a better decision about his offer once she'd evaluated his kissing skills. More than once, she'd been let down by guys who gave great banter but kissed like hungry frogs.

Lorenzo gave a stiff bow. "Madam has excellent taste."

Ryan snorted. "That's debatable, since she's with me. What's a caffè ...what did you call it?"

"Espresso with grappa, sir." The maître d's mask slipped just enough to reveal the shadow of a knowing grin.

A slow, sexy smile unfurled across Ryan's face. "Check please, Lorenzo."

As they walked to his truck, Ryan rested his hand on the small of her back. Lilo's heart pitter-pattered like a tween about to play Seven Minutes in Heaven with the coolest boy in school.

But if Ryan kissed as masterfully as he flirted, there'd be no reason to stop after seven minutes. Giddy with anticipation, she glanced at his lush mouth.

The tip of his pink tongue flicked out to tease the corner of his lips.

Her knees wobbled. She was taking a huge gamble here, and a foolish one. But somewhere deep inside, she knew he'd be worth it.

On the drive back to Lilo's place, Ryan thanked his lucky stars, his guardian angel, and Gemma Moore, Jesse's woo-woo girlfriend, who encouraged him to take a chance on prickly, intense Lilo. So many times during their dinner, he was sure the beautiful brewer was about to shut him down, but each time she left the door open.

Gravel crunched beneath his tires as he pulled into Lilo's driveway and parked beside her sleek red Infiniti. For a moment, they both sat there, perfectly still—no sound but the ticking of the Ram's engine and the distant whoosh of surf. Tension hummed between them. Was she regretting her invitation? Should he offer her a graceful way out, or would she take that as a rejection?

Lilo ended his nervous dithering by reaching across the center console and lacing her fingers through his. "Come on in."

Yesss!

She paused inside the door to kick off her high heels, then padded barefoot to the kitchen and fiddled with a black and chrome espresso machine. Typical Lilo—of course she'd have the best model, streamlined and powerful. As the machine began to burble, she turned to him with an enigmatic smile. "I'm gonna put on something warmer so we can sit outside. Grab some blankets off the couch."

He complied, and a moment later she returned wearing fleece slippers, snug leggings, and an oversize sweater that skimmed her curves and bared her collarbone. From the dining room hutch she took two bottles: grappa and amaro. Once the machine spluttered out their espressos, she doctored her cup with sugar and a healthy glug of grappa, then tilted her chin toward the booze. "Name your poison."

His only experience with that Italian rocket fuel had resulted in a two-day hangover, so—

"Will you still respect me if I choose amaro?"

"Sure." She handed him the bottle. "Wouldn't want you to think I'm trying to get you drunk and have my wicked way with you."

His cock leapt at the thought of just what her wicked ways might entail. "Hmm. Sounds tempting, but will you respect me in the morning?"

She raised one eyebrow. "We'll see."

They moved to the porch where he spread plush blankets on the loveseat while she lit the fire pit table. Pretty damn romantic, with crystal skies above and moonlight illuminating the dune grass.

Lilo sat beside him, her thigh pressed warm against his. Instead of claiming a blanket for herself, she draped one throw around their shoulders and another across their laps. A very good sign indeed.

He sipped his sweet, potent coffee, then stretched his arm over the back of the loveseat. "This okay?"

"Yeah." She snuggled closer. "It's nice."

He bit the inside of his cheek to keep from grinning like a big ol' dork. "You have a beautiful home." *How original. Way to impress the lady.*

"This was my great-aunt's house. I took care of her during her last months, and she left me the cottage. Got an offer from a developer, but so far everyone on this block is holding out." She set her cup on the table and leaned her cheek onto his shoulder. "Can you see the beach from your place?"

"A little, if you're flexible and not afraid of heights. You'll have to come check it out sometime."

"Okay, I will." She gazed toward the distant surf. "I can't imagine not living near the sea. I love falling asleep to the sound of Mother Ocean's breath."

For a long, sweet moment he enjoyed the peace, the warm pressure of her body against his, the delicious suspense.

Suddenly, she twisted to face him, her expression serious. "Ryan, if we try this and it doesn't work out, the rest of the year is going to be hell."

God, she was beautiful, bathed in moonlight, the ocean breeze lifting her dark hair. He coiled a tendril around his finger and gazed into her haunting, moon-silver eyes. "I like a challenge."

Her lids lowered as she leaned into his touch.

"May I kiss you, Lilo?"

Her only answer, a dreamy smile. Soft fingers gripped his nape and pulled him closer.

Ryan had experienced some remarkable first kisses, but this one blew them all away. A slow, gentle exploration, luxuriant, pillow-soft lips, the whisper of breath dancing between them, a low, contented hum deep in her throat. When he teased the corners of her mouth with his tongue, she opened to him on a sigh. She tasted of sweet coffee and strong liquor. He felt himself falling and floating. Only their joined mouths anchored him to the earth.

Lilo pulled back and gave him an appraising look. "You're a good kisser. I've been wondering, ever since yesterday's almost kiss."

Dizzy and breathless, he figured he must have misheard. "Sorry, did you say almost kiss?"

"Right out of a movie." Her fingers skated over his chest. "You know, the moment where the couple realize they want each other." Her touch set his whole body tingling.

He raised her hand to his lips and pressed a kiss into her palm, then the translucent skin of her wrist. "For me, that moment came the first time you walked into the brewery."

She huffed a laugh. "That long ago?"

"But when I tried to talk to you, you looked at me like gum on your shoe, so I put that thought on the shelf."

Her smile turned sheepish. "I'd heard what a player you are, always hooking up with tourist hotties. Figured it was a bad idea indulging my attraction to a trifler like you."

He stroked the delicate line of her jaw. "Appearances can be deceiving. Rumors, too." Though she wasn't entirely off base. Dating visitors to TC rather than locals minimized entanglements that might compete with his focus on Salty Dog. And now, the tables were turned.

"Pretty stupid of me to catch feelings for someone who's leaving in a year." He toyed with the wispy curls at her nape. "Especially since my business depends on her good will."

She skimmed her hands over his shoulders and chest. "We both made my dad a promise, and I intend to honor it—unless you prove impossible to work with. Then again, with your charm, you could find another brewer like that." She snapped her fingers.

"Not one of your caliber." He nuzzled the satiny skin beneath her ear.

"How do you know? You haven't even tasted my beers yet." She arched her slender throat, inviting more kisses. "I can't decide if you're being straight with me or just trying to seduce me."

"All of the above, ma'am." He traced the shell of her ear with the tip of his tongue.

She gasped and squirmed. "For the record, this is a terrible idea, hooking up with a coworker."

"That's what people say." Her skin was so delicious, fragrant and warm.

Lilo gripped his shoulders and pulled back. "Before I open up any further, I need to be sure we're compatible in bed. I know what I like and what I want. Is that a problem for you?"

Nerves tangled with sharp arousal. Usually, he was the one to initiate intimacy, but Lilo flipped the script, leaving him uncertain of his next move. And yet, here she was, flushed and hot and offering the prize he'd craved ever since she stepped back into his life.

With a silent prayer, he dove in. "I like a woman who knows what she wants."

Her heavy-lidded gaze simmered with the promise of pleasure. "Want to go inside?"

"Yes, please." He ran his hands down her sides, relishing the slide of cloud-soft wool over silky skin. Tonight, he'd lavish such careful attention on every inch of her beautiful body, she'd forget her notions of leaving Trappers Cove. In this heated moment, keeping her close felt like the most urgent mission of his life.

Lilo rose and tugged him toward the door.

He followed her down a narrow hallway to her elegant bedroom. Wine-red accent wall behind the velvet headboard, silvery-gray fake-fur blanket on the bed, walnut furniture with clean, geometric lines. Smooth, stylish, and perfectly Lilo. What had she said about the maître d'? "People have facets"—and hers fascinated him.

The candle he gave her earlier flickered in a tall hurricane lamp, its subtle, spicy scent diffusing through the room. Slow R & B wafted from a speaker on the dresser. A grin tugged at his lips. Hot damn! Lilo had anticipated this moment and set the stage for seduction.

"Welcome to my lair." She wound her arms around his neck and swayed to the music. Her slow, lazy kisses gave way to nibbles along his jawline. When she nipped his earlobe, his cock leapt in his too-snug pants.

"You're so pretty, Ryan," she purred as her breasts grazed his chest. "When I saw you emerge from the sea like a sexy selkie, I knew I was in trouble."

He tunneled greedy hands under her sweater and palmed her smooth back. "Good trouble?"

"Very good." Her head lolled as he trailed kisses down her throat, then ran his tongue over the delicate curve of her collarbone. Cupping her bare breasts, he grinned against her temple. "No bra. You were expecting this?"

Her low, sexy laugh gave him shivers. When he squeezed the heavy, silken mounds, her eyes closed on a moan. Her nipples hardening under his touch. He had to taste her.

As he danced her toward the bed, he murmured, "Can we lie down?"

"Not yet." Stubbornly holding her ground, she tugged his sweater up and ran her hands over his chest. "Oooo, very nice."

His breath caught as she pressed her hot, open mouth to the crook of his neck.

"Lilo," he moaned and clutched her tighter.

But she broke away to slide out of her sweater and leggings. Clad only in tiny satin panties, she wound her arms around his neck. "Dance with me, Ryan."

Her silken skin glided over his as they swayed and spun, hands exploring. She kneaded the muscles of his back, then raked her fingers into his hair and scraped his scalp with her nails while her other hand slid down to cup his rear.

Lust reared up and roared. This remarkable woman was stripping him of control—something he normally avoided at all costs. But in her skilled hands, he gladly surrendered. What a gift, to immerse himself completely in the present moment.

Grasping her hips, he snugged her against his erection, drawing a moan from her throat.

"You're so hard."

"Have been all night. You drive me wild, Lilo." He slipped his hand into her panties and squeezed her plump, firm cheeks.

Her finger dipped inside his belt to tickle the crack of his ass. "That day on the beach, when you pulled off your wetsuit, you flashed me." She giggled against his chest. "Did you do that on purpose?"

"Maybe." Really, he hadn't, but why not let her think he was smooth like that?

"I couldn't stop thinking about it." She rained kisses over his throat and chest. "Take your pants off."

He quickly unfastened his belt and let his slacks drop to the floor. The brush of her bare legs against his turned his knees to water, but he continued to sway her backward until they collided with the bed at long last. Nothing separated them but his undershorts and her panties. Fusing their mouths in a deep kiss, he lowered her to the mattress, then knelt before her. "God, Lilo, you're glorious."

He spread her thighs and kissed, nibbled, and licked his way up to paradise, then tugged her panties down with his teeth. She bloomed for him, her folds plump and pink as a flower, glistening with her arousal. Undulating in his grasp, she clutched his hair and pulled his face to her sex.

He dove in, tonguing her in long licks and tight swirls, drinking in each gasp and moan. Her thighs tightened. Her belly muscles jolted.

"That's right, Lilo," he murmured. "Let go. I've got you."

"No!" She bolted upright on the bed. "Wait."

Startled, he jerked back. "Did I hurt you?"

Her beautiful breasts rose and fell as she gulped air. "No, I love the way your tongue feels on my clit. But I want you inside me when I come."

Her lusty command nearly tipped him over the edge. Breathless, he awaited her next move.

She reached down and caressed his aching shaft through his shorts while her free hand fumbled in her nightstand drawer. With a wicked smile, she pressed a foil packet into his palm. While he sheathed himself, she rose to her feet, then turned and bent over the bed, gazing up at him with fevered eyes.

Sizzling with need, he gripped her lush ass and slid home, then stilled to relish the tight, slick grip of her. Pure heaven.

She clutched the sheets and mewled, angling her hips to take him deeper. "Please, Ry."

He fucked her in slow, smooth strokes, trying his damnedest to make this ecstasy last.

"Smack my ass," she growled through gritted teeth.

God, this woman was wild. He slapped her creamy flesh and watched the redness bloom. Her inner muscles clenched around him. "I'm so close. Do it again."

He'd never been into spanking, but her molten-hot reaction ripped away his control. When he gave her another sharp slap, she threw her head back and keened. Reaching around her, he found her clit and stroked it firmly while he fell across her back and pummeled her. With a prolonged wail, she shattered, her sweet pussy fluttering around his cock, hurtling him into a blinding supernova of bliss.

Panting hard, they collapsed onto the bed.

When he could breathe again, he kissed her nape. "Holy hell, Lilo. That was intense." Limbs tangled with hers, he stroked spirals over her damp skin.

"Wow." She chuckled into the fur blanket. "I knew we'd be good together, but that was spectacular."

"Amazing."

"Nuclear-level sex."

He brushed her hair back from her sweaty face. "You do have a certain glow."

With a playful snarl, she grabbed his hand and sank her teeth into the fleshy mound beneath his thumb. "You know," she purred, "despite our differences, I think we're going to have to give this a go."

"Agreed." Reluctantly, he withdrew from her welcoming body and trotted to the bathroom to dispose of the condom. When he returned with a towel for Lilo, found her sprawled across the bed like a well-loved cat, her heavy-lidded gaze following his movements as he dabbed the slickness from between her splayed thighs, then tossed away the towel and stretched out beside her.

"You, madam, are the most delicious woman on the planet." He pulled her atop him like a blanket, and stroked her satiny skin from hip to shoulder, loving the way her sleepy-soft muscles melted under his hands.

He'd nearly drifted off to dreamland when she suddenly popped up onto her elbow. "Hey, do you think my dad left when he did to bring us together?"

Ryan spluttered, at a loss for words. While he loved Robert Eisinger like a father, that's not who he wanted to think about right now. "Does your brain ever stop whirring, Lilo?"

With a laugh, she relaxed into his embrace. "Not really." Her fingertip swirled through his chest hair. "Does yours?"

"You've fucked all other thoughts right out of my head." He kissed her, sweeping his tongue into her silky heat. "All I want to think about is how good you feel in my arms, your delicious kisses, the sight and sound and sensation of you coming apart on my cock."

"Mmm." She slid down his body, dropping hot kisses on his skin. "Want to feel it again?"

He chuckled. "Angel, I don't think I can. I'm not a kid anymore."

"You just might surprise yourself." Her lips brushed his softening cock, and then—hallelujah—she licked his shaft.

Surprise indeed!

Chapter Nine

♥

Lilo blinked herself awake in the pale morning light. She tried to stretch, but the heavy arm draped across her waist hindered her movements. Soft breath tickled her shoulder.

A giddy smile stretched her lips as the memories flooded back—the slide and slap of flesh on flesh. Ryan's hard, muscular body over her, under her, so blissfully deep inside her. His feral growl as he reached his peak. The three—no, four?—mind-blowing climaxes he coaxed from her sore but sated pussy. Truly, the man was gifted. And now he lay beside her, snoring softly against her shoulder.

She'd worried her intense sexuality would scare him off, but he met each challenge with his own demanding need, lifting them both to heights she'd never experienced. Ever. And to think she almost wrote him off as a trifling player.

For a sweet moment, she soaked in the glorious closeness and allowed herself to dream about what could be—a lover she could count on, a real partnership, maybe even...love?

Ryan stretched with a groan and opened his eyes. His smile bloomed like the dawn, making everything bright and new.

"Lilo." He covered his mouth. "Sorry, morning breath."

"Me too." She caressed his sleepy-soft body and dropped a kiss on his nose.

With a sexy moan, he gave her a lingering, closed-mouth kiss. Her body responded, flushed and shivering with pleasure, but he slid out of bed. The desire to keep him there rattled her. Way too soon to have such intense feelings.

"Gotta go back home for my swim stuff." Magnificently nude, he collected his clothes while Lilo drank in the mesmerizing flex of his muscles.

He pulled on his sweater and slacks, then sat beside her, adorably rumpled with his golden hair poking every which way. He stroked her bare skin from shoulder to hip. "Last night was amazing, Lilo."

He chewed his lip, and her gut tightened, bracing for the inevitable "but."

None came—just a wistful smile as he wove their fingers together. "You still scare me a little, but I'm totally bewitched. Where do we go from here?"

Her nervous anticipation evaporated in a flood of warmth. Cupping his stubbled jaw, she kissed him. "We go to work."

"Will we do this again?"

"God, I hope so." She gave his hip a playful smack. "Now, go swim."

Grinning, he rose and backed toward the doorway. "See you at lunch? We'll talk about the Brew Fest." He waggled his eyebrows. "And all the delicious things I want to do with you."

"Sure. I'd like that." Once she heard the soft snick of the front door closing, she fell onto the pillow, grinned at the ceiling, and thanked the angels for guiding her and Ryan together. What a perfect night. What a perfect man.

And her update to the Irish Red Ale was ready today. Ryan would have to admit her tweaks elevated the beer from ordinary to standout. Could her day get any better?

At Salty Dog, after the lunch crowd cleared, Lilo emerged from the brewery to hash out plans for the Brew Fest competition. Beaming like the sun, Ryan waved from a rear booth and patted the seat beside him.

Snuggling with my sweetie at work. How naughty. I love it.

With a giggle, she sat beside him and squeezed his hand under the table. He wiggled his hip against hers, sending sparks of delight right to her not-suitable-for-work places.

Just in time, Wendy sailed through the kitchen's swinging doors. "Hoochie coochie board for two."

Lilo's mouth watered at the artful arrangement of cured meats, cheeses, crusty bread, and pickles. She popped a pickled cherry into her mouth—tart, spicy, sweet, delicious.

Wendy nabbed one too. "Love these little buggers. Say, Lilo, when will that cherry beer be ready?"

"Two more weeks. I promise it's a real winner." She nudged Ryan with her elbow. He knew damn well what she meant, since he had the Brew Fest paperwork spread across the table. "Hey Quinn," she called, "two half-pints of Irish Red, pretty please?"

"Woah now," Ryan protested. "I don't drink during the day. Gotta stay sharp." He lowered his voice and whispered, "Especially after a certain someone kept me up half the night."

She rested her chin on his shoulder. "It was worth it, though."

"Absolutely." Hunger glittered in his eyes.

They jerked apart when Quinn set down their beers and rocked on her heels, hands behind her back.

Lilo slid a glass to Ryan. "Tell me what you think."

The corners of his lips turned down and one eyebrow crept up. "We've been making this stuff for years. I know what it tastes like."

She clinked her glass to his. "I tweaked it."

Jaw hanging, he blinked rapidly. "Do what now?"

"Dad's version was good, but a little bland. Once you've tasted the real thing in Ireland, you know it needs a hint more sweetness and a touch more Irish moss."

Ryan drew back. "Lilo, I'm not serving Irish people. We're lucky if we get visitors from California or British Columbia."

She felt herself stiffen. "You said I'm your master brewer. Either you trust me, or you don't."

"Of course I trust you, but it's not that simple. Before changing the beers, we need to conduct market research."

Itchy with impatience, she huffed a breath and rose from her seat. "Oh, for Pete's sake. Wendy, Quinn, c'mere. She gathered a few servers too, and a pair of regulars waiting to refill their growlers. Quinn set out a half-dozen samples of the new Irish Red Ale.

All eyes watched Ryan as he held his glass to the light, sniffed its contents, then sipped and swished the beer around his mouth. He swallowed and pursed his lips. "Hmmph."

Could he really not taste the difference? Or was he just messing with her head? Seething, Lilo implored the others to drink up.

Wendy slurped, then grinned. "Smooth. Thumbs up."

"Do I taste buttered toast?" a server asked.

Her coworker added, "Kinda like a Heath bar without the chocolate."

Lilo nudged Ryan. "Toffee flavors, characteristic of a good Irish Ale."

"It's bitter, but with a little sweetness." The customer set down his glass and turned to Wendy. "This would taste great with corned beef. You should add a Ruben sandwich to the menu."

Wendy beamed. "I love Rubens."

Ryan bolted to his feet, his face tight. "Now hold on just a goddamn minute."

Everyone froze, clutching their half-empty glasses. Lilo gritted her teeth and awaited Ryan's verdict.

After several deep breaths through flared nostrils, he addressed the group. "Thanks everyone. I appreciate your input."

Quinn shooed them all away and cleared the empty glasses, giving Lilo a sympathetic pat on the back.

"Quit trying to poach my woman, Quinn," Ryan grumbled.

Well, at least he hadn't lost his sense of humor. Maybe there was hope yet.

He clawed his fingers into his hair. "Look, Lilo—the beer's fine."

"Fine?" Her spine stiffened.

"It's very tasty. I'm sure an Irish person would love it. But there's so much more to these decisions than...argh." He squinched his eyes shut. "What am I gonna have to order more of?"

Really? He was going to let pennies stand in the way of beer greatness? She crossed her arms and huffed. "Bramling Cross hops, only a few cents more expensive than what Dad used."

He turned his wary gaze on her. "Please don't make any more changes before consulting me, okay?"

"I thought we were partners."

He rolled his pretty eyes. "We are. And I'm sure my taste in beer isn't as refined as yours. But I've got to watch my costs and ROI. It's a delicate balance, Lilo."

Bristling like a porcupine, she sucked in a deep breath and summoned a vision of Ryan naked in her bed. The memory helped, just a tiny bit. "Okay. Fair enough. But you should know, I have all kinds of experiments cooking."

His fists clenched on the table.

"Don't worry—it's all on my dime. I'm using Dad's home-brewing equipment in his garage." She stood on shaky legs and stalked back to the brewery. The hollow feeling in the pit of her stomach had nothing to do with leaving Wendy's hoochie coochie board untouched.

She'd been stupid to think their newfound closeness would loosen his death grip on his business. If Ryan reacted like this to a slight change in his beer's flavor profile, he'd blow his top clean off when she tried something really interesting. No matter how hot their chemistry, he was still an unimaginative control freak when it came to brewing.

For the rest of her shift, she snuck glances through the glass. How did he do it? While her belly burbled with emotion, he glided from bar to tables to office, his placid expression betraying no trace of upset.

She should let it go, but her anger lent her the edge she needed to persevere. The next beer she presented would be so goddamn perfect Ryan would have no choice but to acknowledge her brewing genius.

Twisting a valve handle, she gave a dry chuckle. "Cocky much? Take it down a notch, Lilo." Though it stung to admit, Ryan certainly excelled at running a popular brew pub, even if his taste in beer was unsophisticated.

She snapped her fingers as the idea hit her. "You want unsophisticated? I'll give you liquid sunshine, baby."

Chapter Ten

♥

Later that night, a few minutes before eleven, Lilo parked in front of Salty Dog. The outdoor seat cushions were already stowed, the propane heaters and fire table extinguished. Inside, servers upended chairs onto tables. She spotted Ryan leaning on the bar, fiddling with his phone.

She rolled her head and shoulders like a boxer entering the ring, hoisted the growler onto her hip, and strutted through the door.

One of the younger servers moved to intercept her. "We're closed, Miss—oh. Hey, Lilo."

Ryan's head snapped up, and he shoved his phone into his pocket. He looked—tired, she decided. Polished as ever, but with a rough edge. He'd been at the bar since that morning. Maybe this wasn't the time to confront him.

He hooked his thumbs into his pockets and sauntered toward her. "You didn't answer my texts. Thought you'd be asleep by now."

"Sorry. Didn't check my phone." She hefted the growler. "Brought you something else to try. Call it a peace offering."

His wide mouth quirked to the side. "Another experiment?"

"This is perfect for summer. I figured you'd want first crack at tasting it. No pressure, no one to distract you."

Ryan lowered his chin and gazed at her through thick, golden lashes. "Of course there's pressure, Lilo." He slid so close she felt the heat rolling off his body. "If I don't like your beer, you'll start looking for a partner whose taste matches yours." He ran his fingertip down her arm. "I want you to stay, but I'm responsible for all this." He waved a hand toward the bar and the brewery beyond.

Her pulse skittered. There was so much more than beer at stake here. She set the growler in his hands. "You don't have to perform for me, Ryan. Just try the beer. I want your honest opinion."

If he didn't like it, she'd pull up her big girl panties and go back to the drawing board. She was an adult, after all. She could handle criticism, even if it soured her stomach.

After a long, intense gaze, he carried the growler to the bar and said goodnight to the night shift bartender, a bushy-bearded hipster. The other employees trickled out as Ryan lowered the security shutters and the lights.

While he worked, Lilo checked her phone. *Shit.* Three, four, five texts from Ryan. The last one read, **For God's sake, talk to me.**

As he approached, his sculpted face cool as marble, she lifted her phone. "Sorry. My parents kept texting me travel photos, so I turned it off. I needed to think."

"Me too." With a deep sigh, he shuffled closer and draped his arms loosely over her shoulders. "I knew falling for you would have messy consequences, but I didn't expect them to start so soon."

Lilo placed her palms on his chest. No matter how sharp their disagreements, she still wanted this man with a desperation that knocked her off-balance. "Look. I should have asked you before messing with Dad's recipes. Next time, I'll tell you what I want to try, okay?"

"I'd appreciate that." With a shaky breath, he pulled her into a hug. For a long moment, they just breathed together, rocking slowly.

Lilo blinked back annoying tears. She wasn't only fighting for her professional future here—she was fighting for his too. And she was gonna drag his fine ass into beer stardom, whether he liked it or not.

She pulled back and cupped his jaw. "Ryan, those Brew Fest judges have sophisticated palates. Salty Dog's beers are excellent quality, but they won't stand out among hundreds of IPAs, Ambers, and Porters. You want the prize money, the accolades, the press? We need something they don't taste every day."

He huffed. "I don't need gold medals to expand my business."

Defensive, much? Entering the competition had been his idea. Still, their budding connection deserved tender handling.

She gently grasped his arm. "Expanding will be a lot easier if you have that stamp of approval. Like it or not, those folks you call beer snobs are key to your growth."

He rolled his eyes. "Okay, okay. What's in the growler?"

"My newest beer baby, Orange Cream Ale. Tastes like a Dreamsicle. It's flavored with orange blossom honey, orange peel, coriander seed, and vanilla beans. Perfect for the summer season."

"You want to enter this in the competition?"

"Perhaps. I've got lots of beers brewing. We'll decide together."

That concession won her a crooked grin. He poured two glasses and clinked. "To the loveliest, most frustrating brewer in the Pacific Northwest."

"To the stubbornest publican on the West Coast."

He sipped the pale orange brew, swished, then swallowed. "Hmm." Another sip. He huffed through his nose. A slow smile bloomed across his face. "Interesting. I can see girls ordering this on a hot day."

She punched his shoulder. "Don't be sexist. I got this recipe from a big, tattooed dude. It was his summer bestseller."

"It's not your recipe?"

"I improved it. Used clementine peel for a brighter flavor and changed the spices." She drained her glass. "Well?"

"It's good. Very summery."

She'd enjoy his praise more if he didn't sound so damned surprised.

He set his glass on the bar, sighed, and pulled her close. "I don't want to fight with you, Lilo," he murmured into her hair.

She rested her cheek on his chest, and the steady beat of his heart eased the tension between them. "I get it. You've gotta defend your territory. And I've got a lot to learn from you about logistics before opening my own brewery."

"Still don't want to partner with me?"

"We've got most of a year to decide." She tilted her face up to his. "Let's not spend that time feuding."

His smile glowed like embers blown back to life. "I can think of better ways to spend our time."

He walked her backward toward a booth. No music this time, just the soft rattle of wind on the shutters. Leaning her against the seatback, he drew her into a deep, sensual kiss, his tongue twining with hers in a silent, heated tango.

This had to mean something, this magnetism that made her crave his touch like oxygen. All her life, Lilo had trusted her gut, and it seldom steered her wrong. And tonight, fate and desire were steering her into this man's path. Maybe Gemma's tarot cards were right. Open mind, open heart...

His hand slid beneath her shirt, electrifying her skin. "Beautiful Lilo," he moaned, "I can't stop thinking about the way you dance around the brew kettles, how you slay me with your sharp tongue and your moonlight eyes." Soft lips brushed over her jaw and cheekbones. He pressed his forehead to hers and pinned her with a fathomless gaze.

"I know we can make this work between us. It won't be easy, but it'll be so damn good. Will you take a chance on us?"

He kissed the sensitive skin behind her ear, his soft hair tickling her cheek, and her last brick of resistance crumbled. "I want this, Ryan. I want you."

"Even if I'm a pain in your ass?"

She squeezed a big handful of his rear.

"Oh, that's right." Sexy mischief twinkled in his smile. "You enjoy a little pain, don't you?"

"I'm with you, aren't I?"

With a feral snarl, he unfastened his belt and whipped it free from the belt loops.

She tensed, but he soothed her fears with a hot, wet kiss to the crook of her neck. "Easy, love. No pain tonight—just pleasure."

Spinning her to face the booth, he bound her wrists to the seatback railing, stroked her hair away from her face, and whispered, "Give me a safe word, Lilo."

Her heart hammered. "Um, Salty Dog."

"Good choice." With brusque motions, he yanked her top up and her bra cups down, growling into her nape as he molded her breasts. The press of his erection against her ass was maddening. She needed his touch between her legs, but when she arched against him, he gave her nipples a sharp pinch. Pleasure zinged straight to her clit. Immobilized by his bulk and her restraints, she could only squirm helplessly, aroused beyond endurance.

"Ryan, please," she panted. "Don't keep me waiting."

His teeth closed gently on her shoulder as he unfastened her jeans and tugged them down, taking her panties with them. Cloth rustled behind her. She shivered at the delicious brush of his chest hair against her bare back. His hand snaked between her thighs to part her aching folds. His other hand grasped the hair at her nape, forcing her head back. "You drive me wild, Lilo," he growled, his breath hot on her cheek. He fisted her hair and plunged two fingers deep into her sex. She gasped as wild pleasure danced between the sensitive points. Her legs trembled. Her pulse raced. If he didn't touch her where she needed him most, she'd explode.

She heard the slide of cloth and the crinkle of foil. His bare legs nudged hers apart. She held her breath.

His hard shaft glided in the slickness between her folds, brushing over her clit again and again. Mewling, she rose on tiptoe and squeezed her thighs together to increase the friction.

At last, his fingers firmly stroked the tortured bud, gliding in rhythm with his thrusts.

"Lilo," he growled into her ear. "Let me inside."

"Yessss," she hissed as he wound an arm around her hips, pulling her firmly against him while his other hand bent her forward. The fat, blunt head of his cock notched at her opening, teasing, nudging, and then he filled her in one slow, glorious thrust. Pleasure pierced her to the marrow, bright and sharp.

Eyes closed, she rode the crescendo of sensation—his low grunts with each dig of his rock-hard cock, the woodsy scent of his cologne mixed with sweat, the roll and pinch of his clever fingers on her nipples, the delicious slide of his skin over hers.

Climax coiled low in her belly, ready to unfurl with one...more...thrust...

She threw her head back and howled as white-hot ecstasy flashed through her, crashing in wave after glorious wave.

His hips pistoned faster. The slap of his flesh against hers brought a lust-drunk groan to her lips.

He chanted her name, then gave an incoherent shout, jerking and shuddering as he reached his peak.

Breathless, they swayed together on unsteady legs until Ryan withdrew and unfettered her. Rubbing her reddened wrists, she turned to face him.

Chest heaving, his glistening cock half-erect, he clutched the knotted condom and gave her the sweetest, dreamiest smile.

"Lilo." He snugged her to his chest and kissed her tenderly.

A fizzing sensation filled her, headier than a Trappist Tripel. "How did you do that?" she whispered.

"Do what, beauty?"

"Make me see stars." She sighed. "I'm talking galaxies, Ryan. The whole damn Beta Quadrant."

Laughing, he pressed his cheek to the top of her head. "You know that streak of light you see when the starship goes into warp drive?"

"Yeah?"

"That just shot out of my body." He lifted the condom. "Better dispose of this. It's probably radioactive."

Giggling, she tugged her clothes back into place.

A moment later, naked except for his socks, Ryan trotted back from the restroom.

Quaking with laughter, Lilo dropped into the booth while he pulled his clothes on, then sat beside her, flung his arm around her shoulders, and propped his feet on the opposite bench. "Well, well, well. That went a thousand times better than I'd hoped."

"Hey." She bumped his shoulder. "From now on, let's do better."

"Darling, I'm not sure that's possible." He kissed the tip of her nose. "What could be better than this?"

"You know what I mean." She squeezed his thigh. "Us. Together. Here. Let's make Salty Dog shine."

His bottomless gaze held her tighter than any restraint ever could. "Yeah. Let's do that."

Chapter Eleven

♥

Two weeks later, during the post-lunch lull, Ryan sat in a rear booth going over Lilo's order for brewing equipment upgrades. Funny, she hadn't mentioned these big-ticket expenses during their lunchtime quickie upstairs. Of course, neither of them was feeling particularly chatty in the heat of the moment, and they'd both had their mouths full. But now—nothing like a major cash outlay to pop his happy, horny bubble and send him plummeting back to cold, hard reality. Even though he was pretty damn sure he was falling in love with her, she was driving him crazy with all these changes.

He got it—her beer expertise far outstripped his own. But her "improvements" to her dad's tried-and-true recipes were costing him money. And honestly, he could hardly taste the difference, though Quinn and the brew crew could.

It didn't help matters that, when she pierced him with those intense, stormy eyes, he found it impossible to tell her no. Whether directing the brewery staff, laughing with the bar workers on her breaks, or snuggling with him after hours, she was so vivid, so passionate, so bright he couldn't help surrendering control.

And that had to stop.

Salty Dog was a success because he watched every detail like a hungry hawk. It was up to him to keep the business humming, and that required a clear head. Just yesterday, a steamy encounter in his office wiped his memory of a drippy sink, and by the end of the day, he had a flooded restroom to deal with. He was losing his edge—Lilo had worn it smooth with her smoky gaze, her velvet tongue, her satin skin.

Great. And now I'm hard again. Holding the stack of papers over his crotch, he limped back to his office.

"Hurt yourself swimming, boss?" Quinn called.

"Yeah," he grumbled. "I'm a little stiff."

As he passed, he spotted Lilo perched on a ladder, fiddling with her control panel. Marco called up to her, his words muffled by the glass and the roar of hot water sluicing into a brewing kettle. As she replied with much gesticulating, her long, dark ponytail swung like a silk curtain over her shoulder. Marco grinned and gave her a thumbs up.

Some discreet questioning had assured Ryan that the brewing staff adored Lilo. Pretty amazing how quickly she'd assumed leadership without ruffling any feathers.

Now, if he could just get through tonight without ruffling that sleek, dark plumage. She'd warned him three new experimental beers were ready for tasting. He prayed they wouldn't be too—what was a diplomatic word for it?—unusual.

A little after eleven, he and Quinn chased the last regulars from their stools. Wendy had locked the kitchen down tight two hours ago, so he was surprised to see Lilo emerging through the swinging doors with a tray of food.

"Don't worry." She tossed her loose hair over her shoulder. "I have Wendy's permission. In fact, she's joining us."

Sure enough, his head cook appeared a moment later. He hardly recognized her without her customary paper cap. She'd fluffed her salt and pepper curls and dusted her face with some kind of sparkly powder.

"Looking good, cookie." He pecked her cheek.

She swatted his arm. "Keep your flirty bullshit for your brewer." She slid into the booth and folded her hands. "Nice to have you guys serving me for once. Now, bring on the beer."

Ryan shot Lilo a wary glance. "What's going on here?"

"Market research." She set down her tray. "Lots of brew pubs suggest beer and food pairings. I want you and Wendy to taste some possible combinations."

Hoo boy. He slid into the booth and braced himself to be tactful.

Lilo projected extra confidence tonight, and not just because of her knee-high boots. In a snug black top and black jeans, she reminded him of a cat burglar from a heist movie. Whatever wacky combos she suggested, he'd do his best to honor her knowledge and skills without endangering the brewery's bottom line. And that wasn't going to be easy.

Lilo stuck two fingers in the corners of her mouth and whistled. Quinn wheeled in a cart loaded with growlers, followed by big, shaggy Marco and tiny, elf-like Mia, the other assistant brewer.

Well played, Lilo. By now, the whole staff knew they were a couple. Pretty hard to speak with kid gloves on your tongue. Quinn and Mia squished into the booth alongside him and Wendy, and Marco pulled up a chair. Lilo distributed beer glasses and hefted the first growler.

"Tonight I'm presenting some European specialty beers. First up, a traditional Flemish Red. Its sour flavor compliments our salmon burger sliders." Her lips tipped in an eager grin. "Go ahead, try them together."

He took a sip, fighting the urge to wince. The beer was flavorful, but definitely sour. Not to his taste at all.

Wendy smacked her lips. "Kinda like a good, tart lemonade. That's a thumbs up from me."

Quinn nodded. "It's good with the fish. Cuts through the richness." She elbowed Ryan. "Whataya think, boss?"

Eight eyeballs regarded him expectantly.

I adore you, Lilo, but I don't like this beer. "It's very, er, interesting."

Lilo's gaze narrowed. She huffed through her nose and picked up another growler. "This is my baby." She held the jug to her cheek as if it were a kitten. "Now, tart cherry beer isn't everyone's cup of tea, but those who like it *really* like it." She poured them each a small glass. "Kriek Lambic is great with cured meats and cheeses, so it'd be perfect with Wendy's hoochie coochie platter. Try it with a bite of ham."

Wendy pronounced the Kriek "genius." Quinn gave it a chef's kiss. Mia gave it a so-so hand waggle, and Marco said, "I'm not sure. I kinda like it, I guess. Ryan?"

He sent up a silent prayer for strength and tact, then sipped. The intense, fruity tartness made him flinch. Lilo's sharp eyes caught his reaction. Her eyebrows tipped up like a sad puppy's, but she quickly hid her hurt behind a grim smile.

Turning her back, she sucked in an audible breath, then poured from the last growler. "Chocolate Weizenbock. See, everybody and their uncle makes chocolate stout or porter, but this is really unique and kind of addictive. We're serving it with Wendy's brownie parfait. Its bitterness is a perfect foil for a rich dessert, and it—"

He nearly choked on his first sip.

Lilo glared. "What now, Ryan?"

Of all the times for his poker face to fail him. "Nothing. Please, go on."

She crossed her arms and cocked a hip. "No, I want to hear your opinion. It's your bar, your business—God knows you've made that clear. So, what do you think of my new beers?"

Everyone's gaze bore down on him, curdling the food and weird brews in his stomach. Forcing the words out was like spitting nails. "Lilo, I'm sorry. For my taste, these are kind of...out there."

Her glare dripped icicles. "Out there?"

"Well now, will ya look at the time." Wendy hustled the others out of the booth, leaving Ryan alone with his furious brewer, who lowered herself into the seat opposite, her body as taut as high voltage wire. She folded her hands on the table. "You don't like my beers."

"You asked me to be honest."

Lilo's jaw tightened. Her eyes narrowed. Her nostrils flared. Leaning in, she growled in a voice he'd never heard from her lovely throat, "Why are you even in the beer business when you don't enjoy craft beers? I've travelled all over Europe learning new recipes. The West Coast too, all the way up to Prince Rupert, B.C., where they make—guess what?—an award-winning Kriek Lambic! And you know what they use to make it? Washington State cherries!" Her eyes blazed and her hands karate-chopped the air. "I've had dozens of interviews on beer blogs and podcasts." She leaned onto the table, crackling with fury. "I know beer, Ryan, and I know what will impress the Brew Fest judges."

"And I know my business," he roared back, at once furious and horrified by his harsh tone. If he didn't pull it together, he was going to lose her, but he couldn't sacrifice Salty Dog to her rarefied taste. If she cared for him, she wouldn't ask him to.

He wrestled his intonation closer to civilized and folded his hands around hers. "Lilo, beer snobs make up a tiny portion of our customer base. We brew what most beer-drinkers want: IPA, Pilsner, Amber, Red Ale, Porter. I'm sticking to what makes sense for the business."

Hurt flashed in her eyes. "That's a big mistake, Ryan. Stick to the same ol' same ol', and you'll never make an impact on the beer scene."

A stress headache thumped behind his eyeballs. "I appreciate all the work you put in, but Salty Dog isn't the right venue for these weird European beers."

Her voice went deadly cold. "Weird?"

That same chill pushed him down in his seat. He'd gone too far. "Lilo."

"I can't talk to you now. I need space." Fists clenched, she rose and stalked away. Every step echoed in his hollow chest.

What a nightmare. He was the barrier between Lilo and her dreams. She should be selling her fruity-patootie beers in some hipster bar in Portland or Seattle. Not out here in a kitschy beach town where people valued tradition over pointless so-called innovation.

He should never have agreed to Robert's scheme. If they hadn't spent so much time together, he'd never have fallen for Lilo. And he'd never have hurt her.

But could he care for like her and not appreciate her beers? Would keeping her require him to ignore his own judgment and common sense?

His heart and his business were on the line. Either way, he was ruined.

Chapter Twelve

Rounding a bend in the rutted road, Ryan spotted Jesse's battered truck parked beside the farmhouse. Thank God—after last night's blow-up with Lilo, he desperately needed a sounding board and some therapeutic digging in the dirt. When a dozen texts went unanswered and two calls went straight to voice mail, Ryan decided to drive out to the farm on the chance his best friend had once again neglected to check his phone.

Typical Jesse. You'd think, after an ignored text nearly ended his relationship with Gemma, he'd learn to check his phone more often. But whenever Ryan complained about his friend's stubborn, incommunicado ways, Jesse would grumble, "Phone's for my convenience. It's not my master."

The greenhouse door stood open. Inside, he found Jesse bent over a raised planter of basil, wiggling his ass and singing off-key.

Ryan grabbed a pair of well-worn leather work gloves and a trowel before stepping to Jesse's side and elbowing his ribs.

Jesse yelped and nearly jumped out of his boots. "Jebus H. Cripes, Ry. Warn a man, why don't you?" He shucked his garden gloves and removed his ear buds, then peered at Ryan through narrowed eyes. "What's wrong?"

"You got leaves in your hair." He plucked the greenery from a curl near Jesse's ear.

"Don't change the subject. Why aren't you at the bar?"

"It's not a bar, it's a brew pub."

Jesse snorted. "Potato potahto. The Ryan Lee I know does not leave his baby at noon on a Friday when half the town turns out for Wendy's chowder."

Even though Jesse was referring to Salty Dog and not Lilo, Ryan still winced. Lilo definitely wasn't the "baby" type, but whatever the nickname, his newly minted sweetheart had dumped him. Or had he effectively dumped her by rejecting her beers? After tossing and turning all night, the details had become so snarled in his mind, only hard physical labor would untangle the mess.

"I need to think, and I can't think there." He rolled up his sleeves. "Put me to work."

Jesse raised an eyebrow. "Okaaay." He tilted his chin toward the chive bed. "Spotted some weeds popping up. Rip 'em out."

"With pleasure." Ryan bent over the slender leaves and purple pompom flowers. Sinking his hands into the dirt always calmed his racing thoughts—ever since he was a little kid helping his widowed mom raise herbs and veggies. Because his apartment above the brewery didn't have room for a garden, he inflicted his help on Jesse whenever he needed to—what did Allyson call it?

"You need to get out of that brewery and touch grass, bro."

In this case, his snarky younger sister was right. He needed perspective. Too bad she wasn't in town to kick his ass around the block. She was up in British Columbia at some songwriter festival, and their older sister Daphne, well—she'd just mouth platitudes about seeing things from both sides.

He couldn't afford to see this from Lilo's side. He had to protect his business, even if it cost him Lilo's love.

Love. We almost got there. Just a few more days...

With a frustrated growl, he yanked an invading dandelion from the soil. But mere weed strangulation wasn't enough. He needed to tax his muscles—and pick Jesse's brain.

"Nice job." Jesse smacked Ryan's back. "You're gettin' your fancy shirt dirty."

"Don't care. What's next?"

Jesse nodded toward the greenhouse door. "There's potting soil by the shed. Gotta fill up the new planter." He quirked an eyebrow. "Fifty-pound bags."

Ryan flashed a grim smile. "Perfect."

He marched outside and hefted the first sack. Woah! He should definitely do more cross-training, maybe help tote the heavy bags of malt to the mash tun. Except, damn. The brewery was Lilo's domain, and if he had any hope of keeping her there, he'd better give her space. Hell, she was probably hunting for a new job right now.

He stacked another sack atop the first one and staggered back to the greenhouse, where he found Gemma, Jesse's new girlfriend, holding a tray with an insulated coffee carafe and a plate of muffins.

"Hey, Ryan. Saw your truck, so I brought extra." She filled a mug and handed it to him. "Hope oat milk's okay. What brings you out here in the middle of the day?"

"I, uh..."

Gemma was a great woman, and she made Jesse glow like a freakin' lightbulb, but she unnerved Ryan with her weird, woo-woo pronouncements.

"Don't worry, love. Ryan will share when he's ready." Jesse doctored his mug with raw sugar, then slugged down half its contents.

Gemma wrinkled her nose, sidled closer, and waved her hand over Ryan's chest. "I'm sensing a troubled vibe. Your aura's dark and swirly."

Behind her, Jesse grunted.

Ignoring him, Gemma patted Ryan's arm. "You Capricorns, always holding the reins so tight. It's hard to let go, isn't it? You're afraid something awful will happen if you're not a hundred percent in charge."

Ryan rolled his eyes. "You've been talking to Lilo?"

Her bland smile betrayed not the faintest flicker of deceit. "Not for a few days. She's been holed up brewing new beers. Can't wait to taste them." She peered up at him. "Ah, I see. You two are sparring for control."

That's putting it mildly.

His mouth full of muffin, Jesse draped his arm around his girlfriend's shoulders. "Gemma knows things about people. I don't understand how she does it, but she's usually right."

Gemma beamed up at the big ox, then leveled Ryan with a sharp gaze. "You know, a Scorpio like Lilo could make the perfect partner for someone like you. She's focused and goal oriented. Super loyal too. And Scorpios make great entrepreneurs. But if she feels betrayed or lied to, watch out for her sting. Scorpios hold on to grudges until the end of time."

Astrology lecture finished, she brushed crumbs from Jesse's beard, pecked his lips, and headed for the door, calling over her shoulder, "I'll leave you guys to talk it out."

Ryan huffed a laugh to cover the quiver in his belly.

Grinning broadly, Jesse smacked Ryan's shoulder. "Read you like a book, didn't she?"

"I don't get it, man."

"Get what?" Jesse pulled his work gloves back on and hoisted a sack of potting soil as easily as lifting a pillow.

Ryan followed him with the second sack and emptied it into a new planter bed, a replacement for one destroyed in February's windstorm that nearly took out the whole greenhouse. "I've never met two more dissimilar people, but you two seem to—I dunno—you fit, somehow."

Jesse straightened, grinned, and used a trowel to scratch between his shoulder blades, leaving a smudge of soil on his already stained flannel shirt. His face took on a dreamy cast. "It's love, my friend."

He leaned a hip on the raised planter. "When Gemma first came back to Trappers Cove, I thought, 'I've gotta have her.' Then I got to know her a little better and, even though I wanted her like I want oxygen, I figured we could never work out. I mean," he scrunched his mouth to one side, then the other, "she's like a butterfly, always flitting from place to place, and I'm like a tree, rooted right here." He patted the fresh soil like another man would pet his beloved dog.

"But here's the thing." Brows drawn together, Jesse pointed his trowel right at Ryan's chest. If he didn't know what a softie the big guy was, he'd be scared. "She's forced me to grow, to face fears that, had she not come along, I'd probably have carried around for the rest of my life." He grinned. "Like your fear of losing control, my friend. You think if you just hold on to the reins tight enough, everything will be okay. But I'll let you in on a little secret."

Jesse leaned in close and whispered, "Shit happens." He straightened and clapped Ryan's shoulder. "Even to a tight-ass control freak like you. Or a play-it-safe homebody like me. And fears weigh you down. So loosen up a little. Lilo's a keeper. Don't chase her away with your uptight, bean-counting bullshit."

A heavy weight settled in Ryan's stomach. *I've probably already done that.*

Jesse was in an expansive mood, unusual for the taciturn farmer. He looped his arm over Ryan's shoulders and walked him toward the door. "Gemma gave me just the jolt I needed. She's shown me a different way of looking at the world, and I'm a happier man for it." He led him back to the shed and loaded two more sacks of soil into Ryan's outstretched arms before hefting four sacks and carrying them to the greenhouse as if they were stuffed with cotton balls.

"And you know," he called over his shoulder, "you don't have to understand everything about your partner. I don't get Gemma's need to travel, but it's cool. When she's happy, I'm happy." He set his load at his feet, then relieved Ryan of his burden. "Besides, when she returns from one of her trips, all refreshed and invigorated, the sex is phenomenal."

Ryan huffed a bitter laugh. Phenomenal wasn't a strong enough word to describe sex with Lilo. More like explosive, a mind-blowing supernova of bliss. And chances were good he'd never experience that joy again. But damn it, she'd backed him into a corner. What was he supposed to do, just turn over the brewery? She'd chase away all his regular customers in no time.

He rubbed his sore shoulders. "You're lucky, Jesse. Giving your woman what she needs doesn't hurt your bottom line."

"True." Jesse emptied another sack of soil into the planter. "In fact, she's brought me new customers I never would've approached if she hadn't encouraged me. Lemme tell you, those woo-woo types buy a lot of herbs."

"It's different for me," Ryan grumbled. "Giving Lilo what she needs could ruin my business. Trappers Cove people don't want fruity-pa-tootie beers, they want good, solid brews."

Jesse chuckled. "Don't underestimate TC, my friend."

But Jesse just didn't get it. Frustration built, throbbing in Ryan's temples. "I built that brewery up from a limping wreck to a success. I know my business, damn it, and my customers. I know what sells and what won't."

Jesse gave a snort. "Stubborn Capricorn. That's the goat sign, right? Suits you, always banging your head against everyone and everything. Doesn't that give you a headache?"

More like a heartache.

"Look, Ry." Jesse clasped his shoulders and squeezed hard. "I don't know what you said or did to piss Lilo off, but you wouldn't be here listening to me rhapsodize about true love if you didn't care for the woman. So go make it right. Grovel, if you have to. Don't sacrifice two people's happiness for one man's pride."

Ryan heaved a sigh and pulled Jesse into a one-armed hug. "Thanks for listening, man. You're a good friend, even if you're wrong about this."

He stepped outside and sucked in a lungful of cold, rain-perfumed air. During the hour he'd spent with Jesse, the storm that lingered off the coast had closed in. Fat drops spattered onto the thirsty ground and drummed on the greenhouse roof. Ryan raised his gaze heavenward and watched the roiling clouds. Pierced by shafts of silvery sunlight, they gleamed like Lilo's stormy eyes.

Muscles aching, heart still a tangle, head no clearer than when he arrived, Ryan climbed into his pickup and steered toward work, where he'd probably have to recruit a new head brewer ASAP.

And say goodbye to Lilo.

No more verbal parry and thrust. No more stolen kisses behind the brew kettles. No more hot, carnal embraces, her lithe body undulating beneath his, her thundercloud gaze laying his heart bare. No more...

His stomach rolled. His vision blurred. His chest grew too tight to breathe. Clutching the steering wheel in a death grip, he coasted to a stop beneath a stand of pines and doubled over, wracked by sobs.

Chapter Thirteen

♥

Her face an iron mask, Lilo waited for Ryan to leave the brewery. Three days since their argument, and she still hadn't found a way past her bitterness and bruised ego. Compounding her torment, her body ached for his touch, and her heart leapt whenever she heard his voice or spotted his gorgeous, phony smile. Staying here as head brewer would be torture, a constant reminder of what almost was but could never be. Somehow, she had to bridge the gap between honoring Dad's legacy and protecting her own mental health.

She patted the sleek steel surface of Salty Dog's new 600-gallon hot liquor tank, installed yesterday. This baby would speed up production, helping Ryan reach his goal of more barrels to sell to thirsty customers across the Washington Coast. Would he thank her for the painstaking research she put into finding the right equipment for this small space? Not effin' likely.

Mia sidled up, holding a clipboard. "So, ah, you and the boss still not getting along?"

Deep breath. Mia's a nice kid. Don't bite her head off.

"I'm not going to talk about my personal life at work." She took the clipboard and signed off on Mia's tasks, scribbling her initials so hard she tore the paper.

Mia eyed the destruction. "Okay. But if you change your mind, we're here."

"Thanks, hon." Lilo blinked back annoying tears. What the hell? This wasn't her first feud with a lover. And as much as she'd like to believe this breach could be healed, she couldn't see how. She and Ryan weren't meant to be.

Just as well. Ryan's absence from her bed left her with plenty of evening hours to create new beers. She had reams of notes from her travels. Next year, she was going to crush it at the Rain Coast Brew Fest.

"Yay me," she muttered as she checked the latest hops delivery. Her hyper-focused Girl Boss act didn't quite convince her heart, but concentrating on work was her only shelter in this downpour of pain and regret. Foolishly, she'd dared to hope she and Ryan had something real, something that might last. Their physical connection sizzled like nothing she'd ever experienced. Ironic that a guy who added unexpected spice to every sexual encounter was so stuck on boring, unoriginal beers.

Not that she was looking for a husband, a picket fence, and two point five kids—but a partner would be so nice, someone who was always on her side.

"Guess it just wasn't in the cards for me," she grumbled as she cranked a dial.

"Easy there," Marco warned as he passed with a sack of malt. "Don't break it."

Lilo patted the tank and rested her aching head against the cool metal. "Sorry, baby. Shouldn't take my frustration out on you."

A scraping sound from the doorway jolted her upright. She turned to find Ryan watching her with that poker-faced expression she'd come to loathe—especially since, not long ago, she'd seen his features loosened by desire as he came apart beneath her, above her, spooned around her... She'd loved watching him come, a memory to lock away for the lonely nights ahead.

Damn him for making her remember.

"Lilo, can I talk to you in my office?

She slid a veil of ice over her features. "Sure."

On her way out, she gave Marco and Mia a nervous glance. Mia bugged out her eyes, a silent plea to fix this mess. Couldn't be fun for these two young brewers, working in the middle of a cold war.

Lilo followed Ryan to his office like a prisoner walking to the gallows. Oh shit, was he going to fire her?

He closed the door, sat on the edge of his desk, crossed his arms, and sighed.

She struck a similar pose against the doorframe. "Well?"

After a long, baleful gaze, he sort of—deflated. "Lilo, can't we move past this? Quinn is giving me hell. Wendy too. Even my best friend says I should grovel."

"The great and powerful Ryan Lee groveling? That's hard to imagine."

He flinched as if she'd smacked him. Time to sheathe her stinger.

"Sorry." She rapped her knuckles on her sternum. "I'm still a little raw."

No poker face now, just dull eyes and a gloomy frown. "Me too. Apparently, I suck at ceding control."

An unwelcome flash lit up Lilo's memory—Ryan tied to her headboard, eyes tight shut and mouth open on a gasp while she edged him closer and closer to bliss. Heat flushed her cheeks.

He pushed off the desk and closed the distance between them. "Yeah, I was thinking the same thing." Chuckling, he ran his fingertip down her arm. Against her will, her stupid body bloomed like a hot-house orchid.

"We're so good together, Lilo. And you're right. If we can both put aside our stubborn need for control, we could accomplish great things."

A tiny tickle of hope. Still cautious, she unclenched her jaw. "Hmm. Never thought I'd hear those three little words from you."

His eyes widened. "Three little words?"

"The three words everyone wants to hear: 'You. Are. Right.'"

His posture slumped. Sudden understanding flooded her—he thought she'd meant a different three-word phrase.

They'd never put a label on their feelings, never mentioned the big L word. Hope fizzed in her chest like a freshly opened keg.

He brushed her hand with his. "Well, you have been right about a lot of things. Customers mostly like your tweaks to the beers."

She arched an eyebrow. "Mostly? Have you heard any negative comments besides your own?"

"No," he grumbled, then heaved a sigh and gazed at her through thick, amber lashes. "Look, Lilo, I'm trying to salvage a good thing. We went from adversaries to partners to lovers really fast, and I should have handled it better."

She took his hand. "You didn't act alone. I was willing." *I still am.*

He interlaced their fingers. "Could you open the door just a little?"

She'd almost talked herself into sealing up her heart for good. Before she could formulate an answer, a sharp knock sounded. Quinn poked her head into the office.

"Sorry, boss. Need you out here for a minute."

He squeezed Lilo's hand. "Think about it, okay? Be right back."

On wobbly legs, she moved to his desk and collapsed against it. A stapled bunch of papers fluttered to the floor—entry forms for the

Rain Coast Brew Fest. Snatching them up, she scanned the text, and her heart plummeted. Ryan had already checked the categories he'd be entering. IPA. Irish Red Ale. Porter.

He stepped through the door. "Sorry, rowdy customers needed tending. Where were we?"

Nearly blind with fury, Lilo waved the entry form under his nose. "Right back where we started, at the place where you don't trust my brewing skills, my expertise, my...anything!" She shoved the papers into his chest.

Ryan spluttered, "Lilo, I have to do what's best for the brewery. If we win or even place, that helps both of us."

"Uh huh. You've been stringing me along, pretending you care about my input. Is this how you honor everything Dad did for you?"

Ryan gripped her elbows and yanked her close. "Will you just listen for once?"

She fisted his shirt. "We could have had something real, something life changing. But your cowardice will cost us both a chance for glory, all because you've got to be Mr. In-Control all the damn time."

With a feral growl, he pulled her into a rough kiss, a storm of anger and teeth and lashing tongues. Her body's passionate response only doubled her fury.

Breaking away, he glared. "I don't want to want you this much, Lilo. I wish I'd told your dad I'd find my own brewer. Then we'd both be free of this pain."

"Fine." She pushed him away. "Dad can't fault me for abandoning a lunkhead who refuses my help. As soon as the Brew Fest is over, I'm out of here."

Feet up on his desk, Ryan glowered. So far, three women had invaded his office to bite off a piece of his ass—first Quinn, who saw Lilo storm out, then Wendy, who got an earful when she brought the brewers lunch. Even mousy little Mia stomped in and gave him a tongue lashing for disrespecting her new boss. Seems he'd triggered not only a split with Lilo, but a potential mutiny.

Should've thought to hide the Brew Fest entry form. Should've known Lilo would spot it right away—those sharp, silvery eyes didn't miss a trick. What she hadn't seen, though, was the email he'd written and deleted half a dozen times, asking to swap one of his three entries for one of Lilo's beers—but which one, damn it? He had to admit, though he was in the craft beer business, he was far from a true beer afficionado. But Lilo was, and now he'd lost her for good.

When his phone shrilled, Ryan braced himself for another round of recrimination. Robert Eisinger's number lit up his screen.

"I am fuckin' doomed," he grumbled before tapping the green icon. "Robert. So good to hear from you. How's the road trip?"

"Better before my daughter called in tears. What the hell happened, Ryan? Lilo never cries."

Guilt curdled his stomach as he explained about Lilo's niche beers and her refusal to let him take the lead. "It's my business, damnit. My livelihood, as well as the whole crew's. I can't risk all this to please Lilo."

Robert remained silent for a long moment. "So, if you make all the decisions, what's in it for Lilo?"

"A paycheck." *Wow, do I sound like an asshat.*

Robert sighed into the phone. "Son, my daughter's a better brewer than I am. She experiments, educates herself. She's passionate about quality, so she'd never push a project that won't work. She's the future of craft beer. All you've gotta do is hang onto her coattails."

Ryan's sigh emptied his lungs. "It's too late. We've tried, Robert, but we just can't see eye to eye." *And I muddied the waters by letting my attraction trample my common sense.*

"I'm disappointed in you, son. Over the years, when I gave input about the beers, you didn't give me any guff. Seems like you're thwarting Lilo at every turn."

"That's not fair."

But what if his old friend's statement was accurate? If Lilo wasn't a gorgeous woman he craved all the way to the marrow of his bones, maybe he'd listen to her suggestions with an open mind. Back when they first started working together, she accused him of being a sexist, and he'd done his best to prove her right.

Shit on stale toast.

He stewed silently until a faint glimmer tickled his brain. The more he pondered, the brighter it flared.

"You know what, Robert? You've given me an idea for a project that just might fix things. Thanks for the call."

"Project?"

"Market research. Give Olga a hug for me." He hung up and trotted out to the bar. "Hey Quinn, do me a favor? Get me twenty phone numbers at random from the newsletter list."

Tattooed arms crossed, his bartender gave him the stink-eye. "Why?"

"An experiment. You still got Lilo's growlers in the cooler?"
She nodded.

"Great. Don't mention anything to Lilo, okay?"
She curled her lip. "Haven't you done enough damage, Mr. Horny Pants? Let Lilo be."

A better man probably would, but he had to give it one more try. If Lilo didn't forgive him, he'd find a new head brewer. But Robert was right—her charges of sexism were a hundred percent justified. He'd been defensive with her in ways he never would've been with her father. Probably too late to recapture her heart, but he could damn sure mend the injury to her pride.

Chapter Fourteen

♥

Lilo yanked open the door of Madame Zora's Psychic Emporium, wincing at the brass doorway bell's harsh jangle. Startled by the sudden noise, Zora dropped the singing bowl she was showing a customer. Its melodious chime rang out as it rolled from the counter to the floor.

Great. Now she was taking out her fury on a sweet old hippie lady. Ryan Lee truly brought out the worst in her.

She sucked in a deep breath of incense-heavy air, blew it out, and gave a sheepish wave. "Sorry, Zora. Where's Gemma?"

"Excuse me, dear," Zora murmured to her customer, an older woman Lilo recognized from the book club that met at Salty Dog.

Eyes narrowed, Zora smoothed her batik caftan over her broad bosom and ambled toward Lilo.

"My, my." She angled her head as if studying an interesting crystal. "It's been a long time since I've seen an aura this dark."

Lilo suppressed an eye roll. "Apologies for the bad vibes. I really need to speak to Gemma, though." *And throttle her woo-woo neck.*

Zora nodded slowly, no doubt mentally realigning Lilo's chakras or some such fluff. "She's doing a reading. She'll be out in a moment. Why don't you check out the new clothing arrivals? We have some lovely boho blouses, and bright colors would do you a world of good." With a serene smile, she sashayed back to the counter where her startled customer gawked.

Grumbling curses under her breath, Lilo flashed a rictus grin at the two older women and did as Zora suggested, flipping through the hangers at top speed. A blood-red peasant blouse caught her eye. She carried it to the mirror, held it to her chin, and imagined how well it would disguise the gore stains when she eviscerated Ryan.

"Too violent for your state of mind," Zora called out. "Try a calming blue."

Damn these Moore women with their psychic gifts. Knowing they'd see right through even the tiniest deception made her feel like a walking mood ring.

Gemma emerged from behind the carved wooden screen that divided the fortunetelling space from the shop floor, her arm looped through a portly, grizzled man's. "Take heart, Gus. I know it's been a hard week, but today's reading was very favorable. Good news is just around the corner."

"Hmmph." The old guy fished a hankie from his baggy jeans and blotted his ruddy forehead. "We'll see about that. Zora, give me one of those crystals to drive the IRS outa my store."

Oblivious to Lilo's simmering wrath, Gemma shook her head and watched the man, a fond smile on her face. "Poor Gus. His souvenir shop has been going downhill ever since his wife passed. I wish he'd just sell the place and relax, but he says he'd be lost without it." She turned her sea-green gaze to Lilo. Her eyes widened on a sharp intake of breath. "Oh shit. What happened?"

Lilo snagged her friend's arm and tugged her behind the screen. "I'll tell you what happened," she hissed, her nose inches from Gemma's. "I listened to your advice. I appealed to Ryan's business sense."

Gemma winced. "I take it he wasn't receptive?"

"Receptive?" Lilo barked a bitter laugh. "He hated my beers. Every single one." She sank into a plush chair facing the velvet-covered table where Gemma and Zora gave psychic readings. "Well, not the creamsicle ale, but everyone loves that, even bone-headed betrayers like Ryan."

She folded her arms over her aching, empty chest. How could she have been so stupid as to think a few weeks of carnal bliss would change Ryan's mind? Truth be told, she was the bonehead for ever believing he really cared for her.

Gemma raked her fingers through her hair. "Aww, crap. I was hoping, after Jesse talked some sense into him—"

Lilo blinked in surprise. "Your Jesse?"

"They're like brothers. Funny, right? Hard to imagine two more different people, but they've been tight since forever. When that big windstorm tore up Jesse's greenhouses, Ryan raced out to the farm and worked through the night to cover the plants and patch the holes." She sat beside Gemma and laid a gentle hand over her clenched one. "Ryan's a good man, Lilo."

"He's not good for me." To her utter embarrassment, a tear leaked from the corner of her eye. She swiped it away and glowered at the purple tablecloth. "God, I've been so stupid."

Gingerly, Gemma put her arm around Lilo's shoulders. "What did he do?"

"You told me to give him another chance. You told me he'd come around. You said his eyes glittered with freakin' love when he looked at me."

"They did. They do. He absolutely glows whenever you come near." Her friend gave her a squeeze. "Please, Li, tell me what happened."

A wave of nausea rolled through her. "After telling me he respected my judgment and expertise, he didn't enter any of my beers in the Brew Fest competition. Not one." Hurt and resentment doubled her over. Head cradled on her folded arms, she unleashed a choking sob.

Lilo stroked her hair. "Wow, you're really torn up about this."

"I thought we had something real," she croaked. "He said he wanted to build a future together, and I believed him. I'm the stupidest of stupid stupidheads who ever stupided."

She *hated* feeling gullible. Even more bitter than her anger at Ryan was her rage at herself for believing his lies. Because a man who truly cared for her, who understood what she was trying to achieve would find it in his heart to cede at least a little control.

But not Ryan.

Gemma rested her cheek between Lilo's shoulder blades. "I'm so sorry. I should never have stuck my nose into your business. I'm usually good at reading people, but I really botched it this time." Her friend's voice grew thick with tears. "I guess I'm just so in love with Jesse, I wanted that same happiness for you and Ryan."

A discreet "ahem," jerked Lilo's attention to the screen where Zora stood, arms folded, shaking her head. "Look at you two. So much wailing and gnashing of teeth over a man."

"Over a promise," Lilo corrected her. "A broken one."

Zora sat and from a drawer in the table extracted a deck of tarot cards. She shuffled as she talked, the swoosh and flutter of cards a gentle counterpoint to her words. "Tell me about this promise, darling."

"I agreed to act as head brewer for a year, so Dad could finally retire and take Mom on the cross-country trip he'd always promised her."

"But you didn't want to."

She sniffled and shook her head.

"Then why did you?"

"Because I love my Dad. And he loves Ryan."

"But you don't love Ryan?"

A pang of grief zinged through her. Truth be told, she'd been teetering on the precipice, ready to let go and fall headlong into love with the man who'd just betrayed her.

"I see." Zora nodded sagely. "Deep feelings bring joy and agony, sometimes in equal measure."

Lilo leaned onto her elbows, her head too heavy to support. "I hate feeling like this—angry and vindictive and bitter. Ryan brings out the worst in me."

"He brings out the passion in you," Zora corrected her, "and that's not necessarily a bad thing. Sometimes we need someone to poke us in our sore spots. Sometimes growth requires pain."

"Maybe so," Lilo grumbled. "But right now, I can't see a good side to this. I have to break my promise to Dad, and I hate, hate, hate this whole ugly mess."

At last satisfied with her shuffling, Zora fanned the cards on the table, as smooth as any Vegas dealer. "Pick one."

Lilo shot Gemma a look, but her friend nodded encouragingly.

"Deep breath, dear," Zora intoned. "For a moment, put your pain on the shelf and ask a question."

Lilo did as she was told, closing her eyes and breathing deeply. To her astonishment, she felt a weird coolness, as if someone had pressed a damp cloth to her brow. The sting behind her lids eased. Her pulse slowed. She reached out her forefinger and tapped a card.

"Very good. You have excellent self-control, Lilo. Remember that. Even in moments of great pain, you have the strength you need. Now, open your eyes."

She did so and glanced down at the card she'd chosen.

"The Star," Zora said with a gentle smile. "Perhaps the very best card for a person who's grieving."

Though she hadn't thought about it that way until this very moment, grief was the perfect description for what she was feeling—grief for the love she and Ryan could have had, for all they could have achieved together, for Salty Dog, where she'd had her very first experience as a brewer, the place she'd hoped to nurture into an innovative leader in the Pacific Northwest brewing scen e.But Salty Dog wasn't hers to experiment with. It was Ryan's.

Zora's warm, pillowy hand fell over Lilo's. "We all experience loss, my love. This card is a symbol of healing and hope, a sign of better times ahead, if you persevere. Let the star guide you to a new perspective, new possibilities." She turned her beatific smile on her niece. "Gemma? Your thoughts?"

"Right." Gemma blew out a long breath. "This card reminds us not to get stuck in negativity. If you can open your mind and heart and be willing to feel good again, you will. You'll heal, Gemma."

"Wow." Lilo leaned back in her chair as a strange sense of lightness washed through her. "Look at me, weeping and wailing like a brokenhearted middle schooler." She ran her finger over the card's design, a nude woman kneeling beside a spring, beneath a bright, golden star. In each hand, she held a pitcher. One she emptied into the pool of water before her. The other she poured onto the ground, where it flowed away in rivulets.

"Look at this." She tapped the card. "See how it's flowing in different directions? I could do that too, right?"

Zora's smile widened. "Indeed you could. That's the wisdom of water. Or beer, I suppose. It flows around obstacles. Water always finds its way, and so will you, Lilo."

"Flowing around obstacles." The corners of Lilo's mouth twitched upward. "I like that."

The star illuminated new perspectives, like seeing her feelings for Ryan as an obstacle she could simply flow past. She'd let lust distract her, a mistake everyone made at one time or another. She'd let the possibility of a brew-loving partner blind her to their basic incompatibility.

But she could look at it a different way—Ryan simply wasn't able to cede control, just as she wasn't able to give up her dreams of being an innovator. Lesson learned. Ryan could never have hurt her if she'd listened to her instincts.

And I could never have hurt him, either.

Because no matter how terribly her heart ached, she recognized the pain in his beautiful blue eyes. He wasn't a vindictive person. Deep down, he probably cared for her as much as he was able. He just loved Salty Dog more.

In time, she'd put their star-crossed encounter out of her mind, and her heart, and focus on her own brewery.

"Thank you, Zora." She reached across the table and squeezed Gemma's hand. "And thank you, Gem, for letting me vent. Sorry to mess up your day with my cloudy aura."

"My pleasure, dear." With a comforting pat on the back, Zora left her and Gemma to mop up their tears.

Gemma pulled Lilo to her feet and wrapped her in a tight hug. "Do you feel better, Li?"

She snuffled hard and huffed a laugh. "Honestly, no. I expect I'll feel like cold crap on toast for a long time. But I will get over this." She kissed her friend's cheek. "Just two more weeks, then I'm off to follow my star."

Chapter Fifteen

♥

A wobbly customer waved a beer token under Lilo's nose. "Gimme another Red Irish, beautiful. That stuff is the shit."

Let's hope the judges think so. She spun to the taps, where Mia and Marco poured beers as fast as she and Quinn could serve them. Despite the huge number of breweries filling this Astoria, Oregon parking lot, Salty Dog's booth at the Rain Coast Brew Fest was hopping. The glorious weather helped, no doubt. A brisk coastal breeze ruffled the awning overhead and wafted delicious smells from the food trucks. Shouts and laughter nearly drowned out the loud alt rock from a stage at the far end of the lot, transformed for the weekend into a giant beer garden.

Between customers, Lilo chewed a knuckle and searched the crowd for Ryan. She spotted him still pacing outside the judges' tent. As head brewer, it should've been her job to deliver samples for judging, but Ryan insisted on doing it. Fine, whatever. She was done tilting her lance at his power-trip shield.

Dapper in a Salty Dog tank top, polka-dot suspenders, and vintage pleated pants, Quinn draped a tattooed arm around Lilo's shoulders. "Relax. Winners will be announced soon."

But Lilo couldn't help checking, couldn't surrender the miniscule chance they might emerge from the competition with a medal. Even a bronze would be a career boost, and God knows she needed one, since she was striking out on her own as soon as the winners claimed their awards.

As Ryan pivoted for another nervous lap in front of the judging tent, he glanced up and caught her eye. His intense gaze held hers until she forced herself to look away. Two weeks after their breakup, she still ached for what could have been. But his vise-tight control never wavered, even if that meant missing out on opportunities for growth.

Flow past the obstacle like water, she reminded herself. Some days, that new mantra helped. Today, not so much. Because no matter how many happy burbling streams she imagined, she still cared deeply about Salty Dog. But every time she glimpsed Ryan giving customers the dazzling smile he once bestowed on her, regret gutted her.

Tomorrow she had an appointment to view a potential brewery site—smaller and farther from the coast than she'd like, but with plenty of parking and space for a taproom. To afford it, she'd have to rent out her beloved cottage to tourists and live in an RV on the property. In a few years, when everything was up and running, she'd be able to return to Trappers Cove. Maybe.

The thought of giving up her home filled her with heaviness.

Distraction, quick.

"You know," she told Quinn as she took the next order, "this reminds me of the Brussels Beer Fest."

"Brussels like Belgium?"

"Home of the finest beer, in my humble opinion." She handed two IPAs across the counter. "It's held in the Grand-Place—cobblestones underfoot, wedding-cake buildings all around. But it works just like this—hand over a token, get a beer." She delivered two brimming

Porters. "Except instead of disposable cups, they serve in these gorgeous traditional glasses."

Quinn chuckled, never breaking her rhythm. Fill, serve, fill, serve. "Those Trappist beers will knock you on your ass, right?"

"Especially the tripels. And no snacks to soak up the alcohol, except this one guy selling little paper boats of escargots."

"Eew." Quinn collected another handful of tokens. "Did you try 'em?"

"Of course. The snails are bland, but that garlic butter sauce—wow! I'd eat anything you put that on."

Quinn nudged her and waggled her eyebrows.

Lilo groaned. "I wish, Q. If I were attracted to women, I wouldn't have to deal with so many male egos."

"Don't kid yourself. Women have egos too." Quinn turned away and muttered, "Like a certain brewer I know."

Ignoring the jab, Lilo rose on tiptoe to check the judges' tent for the hundredth time. "Damn, when are they gonna make up their minds?"

"Any minute now."

"Don't know why I'm even worried about it," Lilo grumbled. "No way a tiny brewery like Salty Dog will place with all this competition in IPA, Porter, and Irish red."

Marco raked back his shaggy mop. "Oh, he didn't enter the IPA, he—"

Quinn smacked his arm. "Shut it, Marco"

Weird, but customers pulled Lilo's attention from that puzzle. She poured another Orange Cream Ale, the only one of her specialty beers Ryan remotely approved of. She was floored when he added five barrels to his inventory for the Beer Fest.

Gradually, the crowd thinned as people drifted toward the stage where prize winners would be announced. Quinn's phone buzzed.

"Yeah, boss. Okay. On it." She turned to Lilo. "Ryan wants you to meet him by the stage. Says he's under the Red Bull banner."

"Me? Why?"

"Dunno. Go find out."

Certain Quinn was up to something, Lilo wove through the crowd. It felt good to stretch her legs after standing for hours. As she walked, she took in all the colorful beer booths. Next year, or two years hence at the very latest, one of these booths would be hers. Already, she could picture her brewery. She'd start with a tiny taproom and a rotation of food trucks outside, then take on a partner to manage the front of the house while she supervised production. Gorgeous macho blond dudes need not apply.

Ryan's mussed hair shone golden in the late-afternoon sun. He stared up at the stage and chewed his lip—a gesture that took her right back to the good times before their breakup. Why did he have to be so damn pretty?

Scanning the crowd, he locked eyes with her and beckoned. "Hurry up. They're starting."

She trotted to his side. "Don't know why you're getting your hopes up. Our beers are good, but—"

"Yeah, yeah. You told me dozens of times. Just humor me, okay?"

She heaved a huge sigh, hating this moment to the core of her being. Even two weeks after their split, being near him still hurt like the world's worst hangover.

Applause broke out as the judges stepped onto the stage. The MC slung his arm around a short, bearded hipster dude. "Please welcome last year's gold medal winners of the World Beer Cup, from Ugly Baby Brewery in Asheville, North Carolina, Beckett and Zoe Monteith."

Beckett took the mic. "I know all judges say this, but y'all, choosing this year's winners was damn hard." His pixie-like, blue-haired wife wound her arm through his and beamed up at him.

Lilo winced. *Great, brewers in love. Just what I needed.*

Ryan reached for her hand. She jerked away.

"Please, Lilo. I'm quaking in my boots here."

"Oh, for Pete's sake." She took his hand and let him lace their fingers together. Why did his touch have to feel so good? Why couldn't he have clammy palms like a normal nervous person?

The judges announced winners, starting with IPA. Sure enough, the gold medal went to a big NorCal brewery. A huge, grinning team bopped onto the stage to claim their prize. Next came Pilsner, Porter, Stout, Amber Ale, and Irish Red Ale.

Lilo leaned onto Ryan's arm. "Damn, not even a bronze." She rubbed his biceps, then started back toward their booth.

"Wait a minute." Still staring bright-eyed at the stage, he reeled her back in.

The girl judge's sweet Southern accent rang out. "And now, we move on to specialized categories. I gotta say, we were impressed by the creativity of you West Coast brewers."

Someone hollered, "West Coast, Best Coast."

Grinning, the judge read from her list. "Best beer incorporating chocolate. The bronze medal goes to Funky Monkey Brewers of Eugene, Oregon for their milk chocolate stout. The silver goes to Salty Dog Brewery of Trapper's Cove, Washington for their Chocolate Weizenbock. And the gold medal goes to..."

The top winner's name was drowned out by the thundering of Lilo's heart. She yanked Ryan around to face her. "Did she say...?"

"Come get your medals, y'all."

He tugged her onto the stage where someone hung a medal around her neck. Dizzy, she blinked out at the crowd. There must be some mistake. She hadn't even entered her beers. Beside her, Ryan grinned like a kid on Christmas morning.

"Next category—"

Wobbly and disoriented, Lilo pulled Ryan toward the stairs.

The bearded judge raised a warning hand. "Stay put, Salty Dog."

"Best heritage European beer," his wife called. "The bronze medal goes to—"

Lilo's heart pounded a drumroll while Ryan bounced on his toes.

"Salty Dog Brewery for Bamberger Rauchbier." She giggled into the microphone. "Sorry to any German people out there. I'm sure I murdered that one. It's a smoked beer. Totally delish."

The stage tilted beneath Lilo's feet, but Ryan held her up as the judge placed another medal over her head. It clinked against the first one, the sweetest sound she'd ever heard.

While the other brewers collected their medals, Lilo hooked her claws into Ryan's arm. "What did you do? Steal my beers?"

"Your dad told me where to find the spare key to his brewing garage."

"He was in on this?"

Ryan gave her a shit-eating grin. "Quinn helped me set up a taste test. We chose our three favorites."

"But you can only enter three beers." Tears stung her eyes. "You gave up your slots to enter my brews?"

He cupped her cheek, his touch warm and promising. "After taking some time to think it over, I realized you were right. We had the best chance of winning with something original, not the same old same old."

Beard dude spoke into the mic. "And now, the best beer incorporating fruit." He awarded the bronze medal to a peach IPA from British Columbia, and the silver to a Raspberry Imperial Stout from Tacoma. Lilo's pulse thundered in her throat as Ryan wound his arms around her and pressed his lips to her temple, whispering, "Please, please, please."

"And the gold medal goes to..." The judge looked right at her and grinned. "Rainier Cherry Kriek Lambic from—you guessed it, Salty Dog Brewery! Y'all are killing it this year."

Pure joy lifted Lilo like helium. Without Ryan to anchor her, she'd float into the clouds.

When the judge approached with her medal, Ryan asked, "Can I say something?"

"Sure, man." The guy handed Ryan the mic.

He stepped forward and faced the crowd. "I want to thank the judges for allowing this last-minute change to our entries. You see, I didn't listen to my brewer. I thought our best chance of winning was what she called 'boring beers' like IPA."

Laughter rang out, along with a sprinkling of boos from IPA lovers.

"But a wise brewing mentor reminded me of something I never should've forgotten. To succeed in this business, you've got to trust your brewer." He held out his arm to Lilo, his smile full of hope.

She stumbled into his embrace.

He kissed her hand. "And to succeed in life, you've got to trust your heart. So I'm sorry, Lilo. I was wrong, and you were right. From now on, I'll shut my stubborn mouth and listen to my brewer queen."

"Aww!" A wave of applause swept the audience.

Lilo swiped away happy tears, then skimmed her fingertips over Ryan's beautiful face.

"Kiss, kiss," someone called, and the crowd took up the chant.

He pulled her in and kissed her with such pent-up passion, she nearly forgot where they were. Until he dipped her backward, almost dumping them both onto the floor. The applause tripled, a joyful din that chased her doubts clean away and blasted her heart wide open.

As they left the stage, the female judge told her husband, "Man, I thought he was gonna propose."

Ryan chuckled. "In front of all these people, without asking her first? She'd flay me alive."

Clutching his hand, Lilo realized the idea wasn't so off-putting. In fact, she kind of liked it.

Medals clanking, clinging to Ryan's arm, she moved to the edge of the crowd to cheer and stomp for the other winners. Afterward, once last call was announced and the beer drinkers dispersed, the whole Salty Dog crew trooped to the judging tent for a reception for all the medalists. Quinn, Mia, and Marco enfolded Lilo and Ryan in a giggling, bouncing group hug, chanting, "Salty Dog! Salty Dog!"

Ryan raised a toast of Kriek Lambic. "To Lilo, the brewer who brought Salty Dog into the winner's circle, despite my misguided, stubborn ass. From now on, when it comes to brewing, what she says goes."

Lilo clinked her glass to his. "No, partner. From now on, we make decisions together. After all, someone's gotta watch the bottom line."

He pulled her into his arms. "You mean it?"

"Yeah. We make a good team." She kissed him, then whispered, "Now let's pack it up so we can go celebrate properly."

"Yes, ma'am!" His gleaming smile warmed her from top to toes and all the way to her deepest, snarkiest corners.

Chapter Sixteen

♥

"Great party, boss." Marco tipped his Salty Dog cap, then slung his long, gangly arms around Mia and Quinn. "We're gonna shove off."

"Yeah." Mia waggled her eyebrows. "We'll give you guys some privacy."

About damn time. But really, Ryan couldn't begrudge his work family their hard-earned celebration. Though today's victory rested squarely on Lilo's shoulders, the whole crew contributed to the company's success. What was he gonna do, chase them off so he could jump his brewer's beautiful bones?

The bartender and assistant brewers headed out while Wendy shooed away the rest of the employees and customers who'd gathered for an impromptu celebration. On her way out, the cook lowered the volume on her foot-stomping country playlist. "Aww," she cooed. "Here comes my favorite song. Enjoy, you two."

While the baritone singer crooned about dirt roads and moonlight and forever, Ryan wrapped his arms around Lilo. She sighed and nestled her softness against him, and relief flooded him like the sweet burn of strong whiskey. His gamble had paid off. Would she be here tonight if her beers hadn't won? Or if the judges had rejected his plea for a last-minute change? So many elements fell into place to bring Lilo back into his arms. Maybe the stars were on their side after all.

She shifted closer, her soft breasts pressed tight to his chest. His cock rose in answer to her call, his arousal sweetly painful. He'd fallen hard for this amazing woman—so passionate, so direct, so demanding in all the best ways. In bed or at work, she held him to a higher standard. He looked forward to the challenge of earning her esteem.

He lifted her chin and gazed into those hypnotic gray eyes. "You want to come upstairs?"

Her lips tilted in a wicked smile. "Yes, please."

He moved to shut off lights and lower the security shutters. "And bring some of that cherry Lambic."

Chuckling, she grabbed a half-full growler from the cooler. "I thought you hated my Kriek."

"It's growing on me." He put his arm around her waist. "The more I taste it, the more I want. It's the same with you, love. The more I get to know you, the more I want to know you. Intimately."

"Is that so?" Flashing a devilish smile, she tugged him toward the stairs.

"Uh huh." He kissed the soft skin of her throat, warm and fragrant with spices and the toasty scent of malt. "I'm serious, Lilo. And I'm not just talking about sex, though I crave you all the damn time. Like, every second of every day. Giving you space has been the hardest thing I've ever done. I want to dive deeper." He stroked her satin hair back from her forehead, then dropped a kiss there. "I need to know what makes those stormy eyes flash, what makes you laugh, what you get hungry for in the middle of the night..."

"Besides you?" Laughing, she yanked his shirt from his jeans and stroked his back, her touch silky and seductive.

He stilled her questing fingers. "I'm serious, Lilo. I'm all the way in. Are you with me?"

A tear slid down her cheek. In a voice thick with emotion, she murmured, "We've got plenty of time to get better acquainted."

The reminder of their timeline tightened his nerves. "Ten months?"

"Probably longer." She rocked her pelvis against him.

"Probably?" He rocked back, letting her feel how much he wanted her.

Laughing, she nuzzled his neck, then nipped his earlobe. "After what you did today, I'm leaning toward definitely."

He grinned into their kiss. "Lean harder, Lilo. Together, you and I are going places."

She threw her head back and laughed, a rich, warm sound that he wanted to hear again and again. "Can we start with your bed?"

Wrapped in Ryan's arms, Lilo tumbled backward through his apartment door half undressed, blazing with arousal, and giddy with gratitude—to him, for trusting her at last, to the judges, for loving her beers, to the stars above for guiding her stubborn, snarky self into this wonderful man's path.

Ryan flicked on a lamp, then started to close the curtains over the big picture window.

"No, leave them open." Hooking her fingertips into the waist of his jeans, she tugged him closer to the panoramic view. "Let the full moon work its magic."

"It already has." He raked his fingers into her hair and kissed her senseless. His velvet tongue danced over hers while his hips rocked in counterpoint, a sensual dance that stole her breath.

She made quick work of his shirt buttons and gazed in rapt wonder at the play of moonlight over his bare torso. "You're so beautiful, Ryan. I've missed you."

"Lovely Lilo," he murmured into the crook of her neck. "I thought I'd never hold you again. That terrified me." His clever fingers unfastened her jeans and slid over her ass, digging in with a possessive grip. "Let's never fight again."

She laughed into his fervent kiss. "I'm sure we will. But so what? You're my favorite sparring partner."

With his help, she wriggled out of her jeans and wound her leg around his hips, grinding against his rigid shaft. God, he was so delicious. To think she'd nearly lost this strong, smart, funny, stubborn-ass, sexy man. Another giggle escaped her lips.

"What's funny, angel?" He kneaded her hips.

"I wonder if Dad engineered this whole thing."

"The contest?" He tugged her bra strap down with his teeth.

"You and me. I'll bet he saw something we both missed."

He ducked lower to tongue her nipple, then bit down, shooting a jolt of pleasure straight to her clit. "I didn't miss a thing, Lilo. I've wanted you for years."

She raked her hands into his soft, thick hair and tugged. "Don't tell me. Show me."

"Challenge accepted." With a grunt, he lifted her onto a sideboard beside the window, the perfect height to align her hips with his. The marble surface felt cool beneath her heated skin, but his hands scalded her as he stripped off her bra and panties. He glided his fingertips over her curves as if memorizing her shape, then lowered his head to lave her breast with his velvet tongue.

"You know," she murmured into his hair, "if someone's out for a night walk on the beach and looks this way, they'll get quite a show." The thought fired her blood.

"Let 'em watch." He broke contact long enough to strip off the rest of his clothing. "I love the feel of your skin against mine, Lilo. Let's be naked as often as possible."

Her laughter dissolved into sighs as he kissed down her front, pausing to lick a spiral around her navel before parting her thighs and diving in with tongue-strokes and nibbles that left her delirious with pleasure.

"Ryan, I want you inside me," she panted.

"And you'll have me, angel, but give me this first." He slid two long fingers inside her and crooked them, teasing that magical spot that made her quake and jolt. "That's it, Lilo. Don't hold back. I love to watch you come."

He stroked and teased her until a devastating climax ripped a scream from her throat and blinded her with pure, brilliant bliss.

Her inner muscles were still trembling when he withdrew his fingers, licked them clean, sheathed himself, and impaled her on his iron-hard cock. For a breathless moment, he clutched her to him, buried to the hilt inside her. Deliciously full, she clung to him and held her breath.

And then, sweet angels in heaven, he began to move, gliding in and out in long, smooth strokes. A second climax coiled low in her belly, ready to strike.

Ryan's rhythm stuttered, then sped. "Lilo, I love you so damn much. Stay with me."

His rapid thrusts pushed from her lips a chorus of "Yes, yes, yes..." until she shattered in his arms, helpless, boneless, lost in ecstasy.

Long moments later, he lifted his head and fixed her with his brilliant, liquid gaze. His lips, swollen and flushed from a thousand kisses, lifted at the corners. "So, was that a 'Yes, I'm coming,' or a 'Yes, I'll stay'?"

Nerves singing, muscles melting, her smile as wide as the Pacific, she cupped his jaw. "Both. I'm in love with you, Ryan. I want to stay." She kissed his mouth, his cheek, his warm, damp neck. "I want to build a beer empire with you and fuck you on my lunch break and wake up in your arms. I want all of it."

"Well, hallelujah." He traced her cheekbones with his thumbs, his touch feather light. "Let's do all that."

"And I want to introduce Trappers Cove to Kriek Lambic."

He smacked her ass with a resounding thwack. "Of course you do, my brewer queen."

She bit his earlobe. "We could call it Up a Kriek."

He groaned. "Weird beer and puns. What am I going to do with you?"

"I have a few ideas." Wrapping her legs around him, she gave him a smoldering kiss.

"I have no doubt." With a comical snarl, he lifted her and carried her to the sofa. "Give me your best shot."

Growling deep in her throat, she wrestled him onto his back and straddled him. "Oh, I will. That's a promise."

Thanks for reading *Passionate Brew*! If you enjoyed Ryan and Lilo's story, please leave a review on your favorite bookseller's website or book review platform. Your reviews help so very much!

Don't miss the next steamy story in the *Trappers Cove* series. Check out Annie and Michael's story, *The Billionaire's Christmas Castle: A Steamy Silver Fox Holiday Beach Romance*. When a control-freak brewery owner is forced to partner with a prickly, seductive master brewer, their business and their hearts will never be the same.

For more contemporary romance with heart and heat, please visit my website, sadirastone.com, and sign up for my monthly <u>newsletter</u>. Subscribers will receive a free steamy silver-fox romance novella!

Acknowledgments

One of the many things I love about writing fiction is the chance to explore all the careers I might have pursued if my life had taken a different turn. So far, I've written about running a bookshop (*Through the Red Door*), an ice cream shop (*Gelato Surprise*), an art/photography studio (*Runaway Love Story, Love, Art, and Other Obstacles*), a tattoo studio (*Opposites Ignite)* a neighborhood bar (*Bangers Tavern Romance series*), a food-truck (*Delicious Heat*), and now a hippie-dippy shop and an herb farm!

I owe a huge thanks to the many professionals who answer my pesky questions, and to all the YouTubers who provide virtual tours of their businesses and passions.

Thanks to Dar Albert of Wicked Smart Designs for her inspired book covers, and to my oh-so-patient husband for supporting me in my writing journey. He says I'm the only wife he knows who encourages her husband to go play golf so she can write uninterrupted. You're the BHE, Babes!

Also By Sadira Stone

The Trappers Cove Romance Series

Welcome to Trappers Cove, a quirky Washington State beach town nestled among the pines. Here you'll find steamy, small-town romance, laughter and tears, Madame Zora's Psychic Emporium, all the best beachy fun, heart-warming chosen family, and guaranteed HEAs with no cliffhangers ever!

<u>Passion in the Cards: An Opposites-Attract Metaphysical Beach Town Romance</u>

Headstrong, homebody farmer clashes with freedom-loving hippie chick, but their blazing chemistry is unstoppable. Though Jesse knows the bewitching fortuneteller Gemma will never settle down in their quirky beach town, he can't resist playing with fire. When a harmless secret backfires, Gemma discovers just how deeply she's wounded Jesse, and how desperately she wants to keep him.

The Bangers Tavern Romance Series

Sizzling contemporary romance set in a neighborhood bar in Tacoma, Washington. Found family, all the feels, and the best tater tots in town!

Christmas Rekindled: Bangers Tavern Romance One

Bangers' bartender River has a damn good reason for hating Christmas, and an equally good reason for resenting new server Charlie—until a kiss under the mistletoe flares hot enough to melt the North Pole. To save the bar they love, these two Scrooges must put aside their enmity and find the good in each other. Enemies to lovers, fake dating, workplace romance

Opposites Ignite: Bangers Tavern Romance Two

A mismatch sparks the hottest flames! Bodacious, curvy, blue-haired, aspiring tattoo artist Rosie is too smart to fall for her strait-laced coworker at Bangers Tavern. But his shy smile and quiet charm disarm her defenses just when she needs them most. Curvy heroine, shy hero, opposites attract, workplace romance

Delicious Heat: Bangers Tavern Romance Three

Bangers Tavern chef Diego meets a woman who makes his heart sing. Trouble is, she's pregnant with another man's child. To win her, he'll have to convince her and both their interfering families that he's in it for keeps. Foodie romance, pregnant heroine, chef hero, forbidden love, sassy abuela

Sweet Slow Sizzle: Bangers Tavern Romance Four

Bangers Tavern's hunky bouncer Jojo has been crushing on server Lana for years, but her sole focus is keeping her orphaned teen brothers together in the only home they've ever known. When their teen shenanigans land them in trouble, Jojo may be the only person who can save them. Friends to lovers, slow burn, single "mom," workplace romance

Cupid's Silver Spark: A Bangers Tavern Romance Novella

Will Cupid's misfire cost her everything? Still stinging from a breakup, Carla Portofino reluctantly lets her bestie drags her to Bangers Tavern's Anti-Valentine's Bash, Cupid gifts her a swoon-worthy silver fox. Maybe a no-strings fling is the remedy for her tattered heart? He seems perfect, until a greedy real estate development scheme tangles them in more string than either can handle. Over-40 romance, Valentine's Day, lovers to enemies to lovers

The Book Nirvana Series

Steamy contemporary romance set in a quirky bookshop in Eugene, Oregon—because bookshops are sexy!

Through the Red Door: Book Nirvana One

Widow Clara struggles to keep her indie bookshop afloat. Professor Nick comes in search of historical erotica from her famed collection but stays for the lovely bookseller--until a scandal from his past shatters her trust. Love triangle, widowed heroine and hero, second chance at love.

Runaway Love Story: Book Nirvana Two

Fierce passion or long-cherished dreams—she can't hang onto both. An ambitious artist and a sweet, hunky beta hero face family secrets, clashing dreams, and a social media storm, armed only with sizzling chemistry and a strange feeling each might be The One. City Mouse/Country Mouse, athletes, cinnamon roll hero.

Love, Art, and Other Obstacles: Book Nirvana Three

Two young artists—one prickly and independent, one cocky and flirtatious—compete for a prize that could jump-start their careers. Their surprise connection sizzles, but can he battle past her defenses and prove he loves her as she is? Rivals to lovers, bisexual heroine, grumpy/sunshine.

***

Gelato Surprise: A Standalone Beach Romance Novella

When her dastardly ex spoils their family vacation, Danielle heads to the beach alone to lick her wounds. Dashing young gelato vendor Matteo is too delicious to resist. He's determined to make their vacation fling last beyond summer, but convincing her he can fit into her life will take much more than sweet treats and summer kisses. Older woman/younger man, divorced heroine, summer fling.

About the Author

Award-winning contemporary romance author Sadira Stone spins steamy, smoochy tales set in small businesses—a quirky bookstore, a neighborhood bar, a vintage boutique, a hippie-dippy crystal shop, a brewery... Her stories highlight found family, friendship, and the sizzling chemistry that pulls unlikely partners together. When she emerges from her writing cave in Las Vegas, Nevada (which she seldom does) she enjoys dance classes, strumming her ukulele, exploring the West with her charming husband, cooking up a storm, and gobbling all the romance books. For a guaranteed HEA (and no cliffhangers!) visit Sadira at https://sadirastone.com .

Visit Sadira on All the Socials!

https://linktr.ee/SadiraStone